The Crossing of Yamacraw

Creasie M. Washington

Selma, Alabama, USA

The Crossing of Yamacraw

About the Author:

Creasie Mae Washington was born in Camden, Alabama. Surrounded by a loving extended family her parents raised her to be truthful, obedient, and respectful.

At the age of four, Ms. Washington's family moved to Minter, Alabama and lived there until she turned seventeen. She later moved to Washington D.C where she met and married her husband. She later had her first child, but the child died in infancy. After losing her husband and child to death she moved to New York City and eventually back to Alabama where she now resides in Selma, Alabama.

Contents

THE CROSSING OF YAMACRAW

1

CHAPTER ONE

Wheeeeee! Wheeeeee! Wheeeeee! There was an ear splitting sound coming from an ambulance as it sped through the streets of Savannah, Georgia. The paramedics were heading to Yamacraw's ghetto. This was only a few blocks from the main thoroughfare of Broughton and Broad Streets. Before that time quiet laid across the ghetto of Yamacraw like a soft blanket. The sun was a globe of molten gold. It shot laser beams across the street, quay and on the trees, burning away the early morning mist. Yamacraw began springing to life. Rust hinges of the shack's door squeaked open as domestics and factory workers

1

slipped onto the streets and narrow alleys to begin a new day. The spring air was fresh and cool. A friendly voice broke the stillness. Dogs barked in the distance and a lone horse's hove and wagon wheels clanked against the cobblestone pavement. A new spirit spread throughout the city, and it all seemed to have happened because of the simple goodness of God.

Rufus Hannibal IV, who would be six years old in the fall, was awakened by cries from his youngest sister, Lulu. Rufus was still for a while, but when his mother didn't respond to Lulu's screams, he opened the door and went in. Rufus called his mother but received no answer. He crept closer to her bed and shook her lightly. She was cold and stiff to his gentle, small child touch.

Rufus dashed from the room and ran four blocks to his grandmother's house, leaving his younger sister in the bed and unattended. Rufus knew that his mother was dead. He had seen dead dogs and cats stretched out stiff, dead. He remembered when he first saw a dead cat. A man had picked it up from the ground and placed it into a trash bin. Rufus told Ma Sybil about the incident. "The poor cat is gone!" Ma Sybil said frowning.

"Gone where?" Rufus wanted to know. "To cat heaven!" Granny explained. Rufus rang the doorbell, but he didn't wait for Ma Sybil to show. He began banging hard on the door. "Rufus Darling." Ma Sybil spoke, opening the door. "What is the matter? Why are you here in your night clothes?"

"Mama is dead, Ma Sybil!" Rufus stated, tears flooding his eyes. "Oh, my God!" Ma Sybil exclaimed. "Child what are you saying? Your mother is asleep that's all. Agnes hasn't been feeling well lately." Ma Sybil's name was Sylvia Anderson. When Rufus began to talk he shortened Sylvia to Sybil. The name stuck through the years. Most of the children heard some grown-up call her Ma Sybil.

When they arrived at Agnes' house, Rufus' two younger sisters, Zenna, four and Rena Mae, two; were standing on the porch in their nightclothes. Ma Sybil led the children back into the house and went directly to Agnes's room. "Agnes! Agnes!"

Ma Sybil called out loudly. But she could see that there was a change in Agnes' form. She touched her daughter, and knew she was truly dead.

Ma Sybil took the crying Lulu from her crib. She directed Rufus to stay inside with his sisters and rushed to the nearest grocery store and called the police.

"What happened? How did she die? What killed her?" All those questions were levered at Ma Sybil, from the large crowd that gathered around Agnes' house.

A slight breeze was blowing and the day became gray and overcast. There was a prevalent haze of grief, aloft in the neighborhood. The police took a glass from the bedside table. It contained some liquid. When the house was searched they found rat poison. After an autopsy, it was ruled that Agnes had died from rat poisoning by her own hands.

Sam Goldberg produced a note from Agnes. "Please Sam, sell Rufus ten cents worth of rat poison. A rat bit the baby last night. I would have come myself, but I have a temperature and the baby also."

Sam Goldberg, and the whole neighborhood knew that Agnes was ailing and some time ago a rat had bitten Lulu. With that knowledge, in spite of Sam's better judgment he sold Rufus the poison. When the inspectors came to Sam's store and wanted to close it, the whole vicinity supported him: Ma Sybil leading the pack. Sam was a good merchant. He and his wife gave credit to all the people in the neighborhood, and they didn't hound them to death if they couldn't pay on time.

During the summer months, many people paid their debt with blackberries, turnip greens, tomatoes, etc. All that didn't sell Sam's wife canned. In time, Sam Goldberg was completely exonerated with a stiff warning. Under no circumstances was he to sell poison to minors.

A sudden breeze conveyed over the quay. The bright sunlight suddenly clouded and a sense of certainty burst through Ma Sybil's tears. She glanced at her four grandchildren. Now she would be their sole breadwinner. Of course, Uncle Albert and Aunt Callie would help out as much as they could. Ma Sybil had the entire burden to cope with until the pension check started.

Agnes' sickness was so devastating that the world didn't mean anything to her. The prayers she prayed availed nothing. Rufus III, was gone. He was gone from her and their children forever. Agnes knew what she was going to do, but no one would be capable of appreciating or understanding all the dept of her anguish. Agnes blamed Yamacraw for the agonizing state of suspense in which she lived. Even her loneliness was attributed Yamacraw. And the rare good moments that came did nothing to soothe her.

In Agnes' room, where the noise came from the streets, she could hear her husband's footsteps coming home. The words of the pension boss that had hurt her most drifted to her mind. Agnes glanced around the room and trembled with aversion. She wanted to die as quickly as possible. The feelings of loneliness, and the craving to be with the man she loved, was too great for her to bear.

Agnes felt humiliated and insulted. She saw from her point of view that she would never enter that office again. She thought for a moment, wrote an address on a sheet of paper and left it on the desk. "When the pension check arrives please forward to this address." Agnes pivoted. She bit her bottom lip lightly. I am not going to faint, she thought. Agnes felt as though she was someone detached, standing off watching a drama unfold. "Oh God! I'm boxed in and my nerves are crawling." She said to herself. She slowly walked away as tears poured from her eyes. When Agnes had reached her mother's house a fresh current of tears streamed down her face. She told her mother what the pension boss had said. Agnes spoke softly and slowly because of the rapid beating of her heart coupled with her fast breathing.

"Don't pay any attention to him, dear." Ma Sybil spoke, her brow slightly corrugated. " That money is for you and your children! Don't let any body keep it from you."

Agnes' sickness grew worse. Every morning, she awoke drowsy. The job that she loved so much, and was proud to do was now detested. In Agnes' minds eye, the men she sold lunch to were undressing her with their eyes.

Agnes stood looking out the window, and could hear the water swishing against the docks; even that depressed her. She tried to think but couldn't. The blood thumping in her ears blotted out all of her ideas. She paused to catch her breath and waited for her pounding heart to decrease its tempo. Then Agnes' mind took up yesterday's troubles. She sat down but her panties were too tight. She took them off. Renewed fear swept her as she tried to think. Agnes' mind was swaying like hungry bats. She walked to the children's room; three were in the same bed. She wanted to kiss them, but was afraid she would awaken them.

CHAPTER ONE

Agnes went into the kitchen and poured Knee-Hi soda into a glass. She took the poison from its hiding place. Agnes went to her room and kissed Lulu, the baby. "I love you Lulu. I love all of my children. But I must join my husband." She said loudly. Agnes remembered when she first met her husband. He was so handsome. And she was so beautiful then. She was lovely and only weighed one hundred and ten pounds. She looked at herself in the mirror. Now, I weigh a miserable eighty-five pounds, she thought. Her mind drifted back to the soft touch of her first born, Rufus. She was happy then.

"Mama, I'm hungry!" The voices from the children echoed in her ears irritated her. Agnes detested the children for disturbing her thoughts. She hated the wail and the touch of the baby. Agnes' state of mind was austere. She felt like closing the door and running away. Her soft brown eyes were constantly stained with tears of grief. She hated Yamacraw; the place she once loved so much.

Agnes sat each day, dreaming about what was. She listened for her husband until there wasn't any sound in her ears. Agnes hated the broken streets, the quay, the river, and the ocean. She hated everything. She wished she were dead with her husband's arms tightly around her.

Agnes' husbands ghost still haunted her. He played Swahili songs on his guitar. Agnes could hear his footsteps coming up the street, stepping proudly with his valise swinging in his hand. Agnes didn't forget God. She knelt down and prayed. Dim thoughts crowded her mind, as if they had broken loose from places where they had been locked up. All rushing toward one goal whirled in her head, blinding her with light.

Savannah, Georgia was the only place Agnes knew. Hartville, South Carolina was less than twenty miles from Savannah, yet she had never been there. Ma Sybil took Agnes to numerous doctors and she was told that Agnes' heart was broken, and her mind was becoming disheveled. Agnes had no will to live, but in time she would forget her grief and concentrate on her family.

The bright sunlight, the sweet smell of flowers, and the gay chanting of the birds failed to revive Agnes. Her mind floated back to when she was a child, waiting for her father to come home from the sea. Agnes' mother had dressed her in a lovely pink organdy dress and she looked pretty. She stood, a small girl on the pier, waiting for her father. And when she grew up and married, she stood on the pier and waited for her husband with their first-born. In spite of Ma Sybil's efforts to revive Agnes, she was still befuddled and filled with sorrow.

Agnes, with her decreasing mental capacity spent her days and nights with her memories. In opposition to Ma Sybil's warning, Phillip Anderson went back to sea. He never quite got rid of the cough entirely and in the spring he caught pneumonia and died. Agnes sobbed and sobbed. First her husband and now her beloved father was dead. Agnes' state of mind to function properly had vanished. After Agnes' husband died, Ma Sybil turned the concession over to her to sell lunches to the dock-workers at the quay. Ma Sybil had operated the business before Agnes was born. Agnes was now, without a husband's support and four children to care for and no job. An exchange at the quay was a good living, at the time. Heaven only knows when the pension check would start and it wouldn't be that much. Agnes delivered the lunches to the dockworkers. And she took the children to the pension office to intercede about the check. The pension boss was furious with Agnes because she kept up the inquiry concerning her husband's check.

"You still coming here looking for a check?" The white pension boss exclaimed. His stout, short body was wobbling as he strode to the window. His huge stomach protruded and his baldhead shined against the sunlight. "Why don't you go out there and grab one of those dockworkers? You will get more money from them than what your check will be, anyway." He said to Agnes crudely. "Pay him no mind." Ma Sybil stated looking over her glasses, when Agnes reported the incident to her. "That money is for your children and you. Let no one sway you away from it."

Ma Sybil mothered Rufus more than his mother did, and he swore never to leave her as long as she was alive. While sitting in the living room one day, talking about someone that was getting married, Rufus said, "I know who I'm going to marry when I grow up. "Who?" His grandfather asked. "Ma Sybil." Rufus said sincerely. The entire family laughed. Rufus sat sheepishly, head down knowing what he had said was wrong. "No, you will not. Ma Sybil is my wife. You have to find your wife", Grandpa Phillip exclaimed. He pulled Rufus over to him and sat him on his knee. "You love Ma Sybil very much, don't you? Grandpa Phillip asked kissing Rufus on the head.

"Yes, I love Ma Sybil." Rufus confessed, looking a little sad. "I love Ma Sybil too." Grandpa stated, still holding Rufus and smiling broadly. "Rufus you can't marry anyone in your family. You must marry someone who isn't related to you.

Cheer up, okay?" Rufus answered okay, sliding from his grandfather's lap.

Agnes thought of those family episodes all the time and felt lonely. One day she knew what she was going to do, but no one would be capable of appreciating her decision. "God will forgive me. I've asked Him to." She said to herself. Agnes wanted to swallow the poison down, right away. She felt a sensation similar to the feeling she got when she breastfed her babies. Before Agnes drank the poison, she prayed for her husband, her father, herself and her family. This brought back memories from her childhood. Suddenly, the darkness that had enveloped her, lifted. For an instant, life glowed before her with all its past joys.

Agnes didn't take her eyes off the poison in the glass. This experience was harsh and painful as in other moments of her life. Like something majestic her soul soared to heights it had never attained before. After a while, reason lagged behind, unable to keep up.

CHAPTER ONE

Agnes spoke with difficulty. Her lips trembled and her face contorted, turning red. "What is life?" Agnes asked herself. An echo penetrated her ears. "Life is pain. Pain in some form from the day you cry until the day you die." This propelled Agnes to swallow the poison. Afterwards, she was horror stricken at what she had done. The pain and dizziness caused her arms to flay about.

Agnes didn't have the strength to cry out or didn't want to cry out. Where am I? Why? Why? Why? She thought. Agnes tried to get up from the bed and go to the bathroom to bring the poison up. At that moment, something flared up like a thunderbolt. It struck Agnes in the head and she fell back onto the bed. "God, please forgive me for everything!" Agnes mumbled, feeling the despair of her body struggling against the poison. A light illuminating her had been shrouded in darkness. It flickered, grew dim, and went out forever.

2

CHAPTER TWO

Ma Sybil was always busy. By nature, she was a workaholic. Ma Sybil's image would always remain vivid and untarnished in Rufus' mind. Ma Sybil nurtured all the children, but she was particularly attached to Rufus. She realized he was sensitive with a high strong nature. And she tried to protect him.

Ma Sybil occasionally glanced up from her work at the four children scattered about the living room. She could see what each one of them would be. Rufus will be the bulwark, the one likely to follow in the Anderson's tradition of stability. He would be a good worker and a guidepost.

CHAPTER TWO

Ma Sybil glanced at the second child, Zenna. She was intermittently, loudly spelling out words and asking for their pronunciations. Zenna will be the bookworm, she thought. Zenna loved books and could read better than Rufus. She seemed older and wiser than all the children. "I'm so glad the child loves books." Ma Sybil thought. "Books give us a deeper consciousness of God. We should grow in our esteem that God's power is part of our being every day. It doesn't matter where we are."

Ma Sybil's eyes picked up the third child, Rena Mae Hannibal. She was pert, and pretty as a fully bloomed pin rose. All the children were comely, but Rena Mae was the beauty of the family. She will be a flirt. An attention seeker, and might live the life of a gypsy, she thought. She won't give a damn about authenticity, virtue, or anything. As Ma Sybil glanced in Rena Mae's direction, she was dismembering a rag doll.

"Rena Mae! Why are you tearing that doll apart?" Ma Sybil asked. "I'm making her better." I don't like her the way she is." Rena Mae said still dismantling the doll. "You best to make her better." Ma Sybil spoke sternly. "If you don't, you will never get another doll from me."

Ma Sybil turned her attention to Lulu, the youngest child. Three years old, jabbering happily in her rocker. Lulu will be easy going, intelligent, and a little slow to grasp things. But, once she learns it, it will stay with her forever. Her husband will be good to her, but may dominate her, she thought.

Rufus had developed a feeling of insecurity. He was afraid, that one day when he awoke, Ma Sybil would also be dead. Once again, he and his sisters would be placed into a home. Although Uncle Albert and Aunt Callie had no children, Rufus didn't believe that they would keep them. Rufus prayed all the time that Ma Sybil would live until he was grown. Rufus became very sensitive and developed an unhealthy attitude. School did not hold much interest for him.

One night, Rufus dreamt that Ma Sybil had died. The social worker came and placed them into different homes. In

Rufus' dream, he was trying to find his sisters. He scaled to the top of a tall iron fence, as he descended, his shirttail was caught on the fence. He was hanging, dangling, and screaming. Rufus was awakened by Zenna forcefully shaking him.

Rufus III remembered his father and grandfather's stories about New Delhi, India. Rufus Hannibal I, was appalled by the living conditions in New Delhi and he broke all ties with his homeland. He refused to speak his native tongue. His family already spoke English and they learned Swahili. That was before Mahatma Gandhi helped to eradicate to the caste system.

When Rufus Hannibal II, was a small boy, his family migrated to Mombassa, Kenya. Rufus Hannibal I grew up in the caste system. One day an English entrepreneur asked for volunteers to travel to East Africa to plant sisal trees. Rufus I, accepted at once, and took his family to Mombassa. Rufus II was a small boy, but he remembered the trip. He had asked his father many times, "When are we going to get there?" When they arrived in Kenya, they settled in the suburbs of Mombassa. Rufus

I, also recalled playing at Fort-Jesus. When he was older, he sold ice cream and other goodies to the tourists.

Rufus Hannibal II met and married the daughter of a leading politician from Nairobi, Kenya. The African family and the New Delhi family produced Rufus Hannibal III. He was very imposing. He could have been one of the proud, lion killing warriors. Rufus Hannibal III had doleful eyes, which seemed out of place on the tall, dignified man. He also had a thick smile, showing lovely pearly white teeth and pink gums. When he chuckled, little crow's feet gathered at the corners of his eyes.

When he was of age, Hannibal III, enrolled at the University of Madrid, Spain. He majored in Political Science, but became bored with his studies and was the first to travel. He signed on as the second-cook on an American ship. Phillip Anderson, the chief cook on that ship, took Hannibal III under his command. Phillip taught Rufus many things about cooking and serving the American way. They became good friends. Phillip

CHAPTER TWO

lip painted a picture of American sights. Rufus enlightened Phillip about the interior of East Africa and its people.

When the ship returned to Savannah, Georgia, Phillip took Rufus to his home and introduced him to the family. For a brief moment, Rufus and Agnes' eyes met and locked; neither was able to look away. It was love a first sight. One year later, Rufus and Agnes were married. Ten months later, Rufus Hannibal, IV was born.

Rufus IV, remembered his father, a tall handsome man. Many times, his father took him for walks around Yamacraw. When he was tired his father gave him a ride home on his shoulders. They also played handball together and Rufus III took his son shopping at Yacham and Yacham Department Store and bought the clothes he needed.

Rufus IV, looked forward to his father coming home from the sea. His father brought them handmade gifts made in Africa and every place they sailed. He enjoyed spending time with his father and learning new words in Swahili. Rufus had told his family that when his baby was born, he was going to take them to Kenya to meet the rest of his family. Rufus III wanted to show his wife and son the interior of Kenya: The Great Rift Valley area, the Kilimanjaro Mountains, the tallest in the country, and the Massa people, who refused to change from their traditional mode of living.

Rufus and Agnes had seven years of total bliss. Rufus was the sea going breadwinner and Agnes, mother and house-wife. Agnes also helped Ma Sybil prepare and deliver the lunches for the dockworkers.

One month before Hannibal and Agnes' fourth child was to be born, Agnes received a telegram stating that Rufus was lost at sea. It had been a terrible storm and the ship was practically destroyed. Most of the crew was lost. However, her father, Phillip Anderson was one of the survivors; but he developed bronchitis and died in the spring.

"Why didn't daddy swim to safety? Grandpa Phillip did." Rufus asked his mother, his eyes swinging back in their sockets.

"Grandpa Phillip was picked up later, drifting in a life-boat." Agnes spoke tearfully. "But they couldn't find your father. Now Rufus, you're the man of the house and you must always look after your sisters."

"Hey Sonny"! A black man called from a candy store. "Do you want to make fifty cents?" Rufus snapped out of his thoughts about his parents when he heard the man mention money.

"Yes sir!" Rufus answered, dropping his hands to his side releasing the blade of grass he had been playing with. Ma Sybil had sent Rufus on an errand and he hopped and skipped as he went.

"Take this package to that car." The man pointed to a black Cadillac on the next block. "Give this parcel to the man sitting at the wheel. I'll give you fifty cents when you get back. Hurry! Hurry!" The man instructed. The heat was on for the Bolita runner.

The next day, Rufus went back to the candy store and asked the man if he needed any packages delivered. Rufus stood breathless, waiting for an answer. The man replied, "No." "Okay." Rufus said as he damned the man in his heart and slowly walked away. Rufus wanted the money for Ma Sybil. He knew that she could buy something with the money or use it to help with the family budget.

Rufus' brown eyes trailed the floating clouds as they took shape in the sky. He was ten years old and unhappy. He sat on a barrel in front of the grocery store where he worked part-time. The main cause of Rufus' unhappiness was his loneliness and recurring thoughts of his dead parents. Rufus sat tapping both sides of the barrel, like a drum, to a Swahili tune that his father had played on his guitar.

Unhappiness laid on Rufus like a cumbersome, inflexible steelyard. Every fiber on his body rebelled against Yamacraw's heavy populated area. Yamacraw was brimming over with people, cats, dogs, and faces, buzzing with flattery and cynicism. No wonder his mother took her life, he thought. "But I wouldn't do that. It must be a better way somewhere in the world." He said to himself. And he was determined that when he had grown up, he was going to find out.

"Stop dreaming Rufus!" Daniel, his black boss yelled, smiling faintly. "Take this nickel piece of ice to this number."

"Yes sir!" Rufus' agile feet began to move with the ice. The ice was neat rows, covered with newspaper and croaker sacks. Rufus pushed the ice onto an old wobbly carriage that he built from discarded baby carriages. As he shoved the ice, his mind picked up where he had left off. His mood of depression heightened until it engulfed him. A swelling arose in his throat and his eyes clouded over. He became confused, passed the house and had to turn back. At that moment, with all his heart he yearned for his grandmother, who had given him the only real mothering he had known.

Rufus had to deliver orders. After his father and grandfather died his mother and grandmother said he was the man of the house; and they needed the money. If he went home to be consoled by Ma Sybil, he could be fired. Many boys his age would be glad to have his job. As he worked he thought of his oldest sister, Zenna. She was his best friend and companion, he couldn't tell her things like he could tell Ma Sybil; she wouldn't understand. So, Rufus tearfully staggered from door to door with his wares.

Ma Sybil's husband, Phillip Anderson, wasn't from the ghetto of Yamacraw. He was born and raised in West Savannah. Phillip was an only child. His mother taught Latin and his father taught mathematics. When he had finished tenth grade, no entreating could get Phillip to continue his studies. He said he wanted to see the world and took a tour as a merchant seaman.

When Phillip's parents died, he sold the house and brought a large house in Yamacraw. Phillip Anderson was a seaman and many of his sea-going partners came from other areas, and had a hard time finding rooms near the dock. Phillip bought the house for his friends and co-workers. The house was walking distance from the dock. Oliver Cransberry and his wife were caretakers for Phillip.

Phillip Anderson met Sylvia Moore one Sunday when he visited her church. Phillip was brought up in the Baptist faith and joined Sylvia's church. They had a courtship for sometime, fell in love, and got married. Albert was their first-born and three years later Agnes was born. Sylvia never worked outside of the home. I must be home to attend to my family, she would say. There wasn't much money in the house that the children knew about. Their cozy, humble house was always spotlessly clean and the lively children were always neat. Albert and Agnes inherited Ma Sybil's passion for cleanliness. Rufus was careful of his clothes and other belongings. He had few playmates during the time he attended school. His clean, neat, second-hand clothes made him feel and look out of place with his dirty, rag-a- muffin schoolmates. Ma Sybil instilled in the children to keep a clean body and mind. Rufus' schoolmates conspired together against him and regarded him as snooty. Rufus was ill prepared to meet the tough kids at school. He never started a fight, but gave a good account of himself if he was attacked. Rufus learned that in order to command respect and make one's existence endurable one had to fight.

Rufus had plenty of courage and soon the bullies learned to leave him alone. Uncle Albert would come every week. He gave each child a dime and Ma Sybil some money to help out. "There are so many things to spend money for. You need money for the doctor. The clinic isn't any good. They only give aspirins. A person must have a nest egg. I want my family put away nicely when they die. So you must have a burial policy," Ma Sybil stated.

Rufus IV, and his sister were from an established Savannah, Georgia family. Most of their relatives were handsome, banana colored, sharp eyed, erect people who clothed themselves in a manner of being special; with no thought whatsoever that they could be otherwise. Although, they lived in the slums of Yamacraw, they didn't live like slum folks. The house was always clean, and when he was away from the sea, he and his friends painted their house.

Their surroundings were always sanitary and pleasant. A large screened-in front porch was used as a living room during the summer. A lovely, Magnolia Tree graced the front yard and a huge Crape Myrtle, shaped and beautified the backyard. The backyard was enclosed with a tall, wooden fence. An alley ran behind the fence. They had eight bedrooms, a living room, dining room, kitchen and library. The library was responsible for Zenna's advanced learning. She was the only one in the family who finished high school. Just about five blocks from the viaduct, with its millions of lights illuminating the pink house at 24 Zubly Street, where the family lived.

Twilight was beginning. The wind ruffled the early morning clouds massing the sky. The clouds were deep purple shared into an ashy lilac. Through the deluge of sunrise, beams poured in a yam-yellow of sunrays, sprawling out like a giant fan. Edna's husband, Oliver Cransberry, was a good-natured person. He was a plumber, with two front teeth missing. And when he laughed, you got the feeling that suddenly a bird would fly out of his mouth. When he walked, he favored his heels. As you watched him ambling along it seemed as though he would stop abruptly.

Oliver and Edna were good people and worked for Grandpa Phillip before he married Ma Sybil. They were neighbors and church sisters. Edna also helped Ma Sybil with the cooking for the dockworkers. Edna, short and stout, was a very cheerful person. When she laughed, it seemed as if the whole world lit up. When most people heard her laugh, they giggled too, although they didn't know what she was laughing about. Edna also took in wash from white people to help with the household needs. Oliver built a shed in the backyard so that his wife could cook the clothes, even if it rained. The big, black, iron pot that was left over from slavery time was emitting billows of smoke that fraternized with the quay's fog.

CHAPTER TWO

Oliver and Edna's only child died of influenza when she was a baby. Every working day, Oliver drove his green Ford truck loaded with co-workers. Almost every person in Yamacraw had pressed his or her seat in Oliver's car.

In the spring, on Saturday mornings, Oliver, his wife Edna, Ma Sybil, and as many children as could fit into the old Ford, went berry picking near the Savannah Sugar Refinery. The children looked forward to those outings. Every morning the children would position themselves on the street corners and wait. When the car was packed to its capacity, some of the children were left on the sidewalk, crying. "Why don't some of you children who come often give another child a chance to pick berries today?" Ma Sybil would ask. Rufus and Zenna had willingly given up their places in the car. Rena Mae never would. "I'm going!" she shouted, jumping up and down on her long skinny legs, engaged in a tantrum that belonged in the nursery.

Spring was well advanced. The children were excited. They greeted the trees and grass with delight. They were awed with the wide-open space revealing colorful houses, manicured lawn, and botany as a whole.

Children ran about in bands. They had a collective enthusiasm as a gang of schoolboys, who were about to swoop on an orchard. Their group went under full steam. Their sun burnt bodies and their bare feet slapped along the ground, lightly pressing down young, green, over-grown, grassy earth. The grass crept inexorably after them, and a soft electrifying wind pervaded. Although Rena Mae was indifferent, she was a good berry picker. And the first berry that she picked, she ate. She picked hurriedly, gulped ravishingly and simultaneously filled her basket.

After Rena Mae's stomach was filled with succulent berries, her basket yielded quicker than the others. When the children's appetites and containers were satisfied, they would wonder into the thickets to find a stream. As they walked, a cautious warning from Ma Sybil went flying after them to be careful of snakes.

CHAPTER TWO

The children could see the squirrels bounding over the grounds, scattered with broken twigs that they hung like museum trapping from branches of Behemoth Sweet Gum Trees. The fury of animals peered around curiously at the invaders, twitching their noses inquiring, indicating that their private territory was being stormed.

The aged, scaled, Sweet Gum Tree with maple like leaves and bark exuded a fragrant substance. The Urchins chewed the hardened sap of the trees as though it was spearmint gum. They scrutinized the split in the tree's trunk and wondered how it got there. The group of Urchins hopped up and down on the giant exposed roots of the tree with green shoots sprouting out on it. They watched as a colony of small ants with bits of food in their mounts marched in and out of a hole in the tree trunk. And they listened to the jaybirds coloratura in the distance. The jaybirds gazed intensely at their target, as they swooped down and settled in the big tree. The kids threw stones into the water and observed the ripple as the marine animals scattered. The gang waded into the pond and caught a small fish, but while purring over it, the slippery thing floundered back into the water.

Suddenly, like a summer storm that blew out over the universe, the pleasant rhythm of the day was shattered. "Time to go home," Ma Sybil called out. The temperature had risen and the hot sand was so intense, that the bare-feet children had to balance on their heels to walk.

After one of their berry-picking outings, Rufus expressed excitingly, "Ma Sybil! I wish we lived out here!" Rufus loved picking berries near the Savannah Sugar Refinery because he saw and admired the lovely homes with large well-groomed lawns and smooth sidewalks. Ma Sybil told him that black people owned houses in that section. Some of Ma Sybil's church members lived there. "Ma Sybil! Why don't we live out there?" He asked.

"If your parents had lived, I'm sure they would've brought a house here," she said. "But I was born in Yamacraw. I have lived there all of my life. I'm an old woman now and I'm sure I'll die there. I never had any thoughts of living any place else. I'm sure it's too late for me, but not for you, Rufus. When you grow up and marry, you probably will buy a house out here."

"Yes, I hope so," Rufus said, smiling. "I like it out here." This is how to live, he thought. Rufus couldn't see any beauty in Yamacraw, other than their house and its surroundings. The scraggy dogs and cats digging, fighting, while over-turning garbage cans for the little scraps.

"Oh! Why did your Western Indian father drown and leave me with these young children?" Ma Sybil always said when the children asked curious questions that they couldn't understand the complete implication. Rufus always chuckled when Ma Sybil made that statement. Because he knew that Ma Sybil knew his father was from East Africa, and had the papers to prove it.

Rufus thought that when he grew-up, he would visit his grandparents in Mombassa. But after his mother died, Ma Sybil made photos of them and sent to Mombassa to their other grandparents. But after they didn't reply, Rufus changed his mind. Maybe they were dead, he thought; but the letters were never returned. Rufus still remembered some Swahili words his father had taught him. Kwa heri means goodbye. Starehe means don't get up or take it easy.

Conditions during The Depression in Yamacraw were at its lowest. People were constantly struggling against misery, hunger, loneliness, and unhappiness that went hand in hand with hard times. But Zenna was content with her lot and she gladly helped as much as she could. She sewed garments for the family and the neighbors, anything that would ease Ma Sybil's burden. Rufus and his sisters weren't hungry, Ma Sybil saw to that. There was always enough to eat in the house, but they couldn't waste anything. Zenna had a second-hand typewriter and when she graduated from high school, Ma Sybil bought her a new machine. Zenna was thankful and proud of the gift, it helped her to keep Ma Sybil's books. Ma Sybil wanted to give her that particular responsibility in the hopes that it would urge her on. But she didn't need urging. Zenna had it in her to be aggressive, proud and ambitious.

Rena Mae, on the other hand, was strange. She had revolting habits that showed up as a child when she was provoked. Her mouth was like a sewer. Four-letter words like acid rain flew in all directions. No one in the family used those words except Rena Mae.

Ma Sybil and Edna, their next-door neighbor, had tried to curb Rena Mae's behavior by washing her mouth with soap. But when she was riled up, the words still flew in all routes. Rena Mae's gutter-mouth aggressiveness was her chlorine gas and her toughness was her armor. People would stare; shake their heads and say, "How such dirty words can come from such a pretty girl?"

Indeed, Rena Mae was a strange person in many ways. When dinner was served, Rena Mae wolfed everything on her plate, and then asked for seconds. "That's all there is." Ma Sybil would say. "Well, I'll have a peanut butter and jelly sandwich. There's plenty of that." Rena Mae would push trying Ma Sybil's mental power. "No, you won't have a sandwich!" Ma Sybil would shout. "You've had your share and more than the rest! That's all for now! Rena Mae would excuse herself. Her entire five feet, eight inches would sulk, and slink from the table. She would smack her lips and issue a clicking sound with her mouth. That was one the most disrespectful acts a black southern child could foster upon one's parents. And she got her fanny smacked.

Rena Mae was a decisive gourmet, but abhorred culinary activities. Ma Sybil had no intentions of permitting her to shirk her duties. Ma Sybil rotated the dishwashing between the two girls. Zenna's were fine, but Rena Mae's were sticky and abrasive, and she had to wash them again. Ma Sybil decided to spy on Rena Mae, to see how she cleaned the dishes. When Ma Sybil saw what Rena Mae was doing, she was shocked and couldn't believe what her eyes were telling her. She took off her glasses and gave them a good cleansing with her apron. Rena Mae was standing at the kitchen sink, carefully and diligently licking each plate and stacking them one by one to dry. "What are you doing Rena Mae?" Ma Sybil shouted as a plate shattered to the floor. Ma Sybil strode closer to the sink as Rena Mae cringed with fear. "Out this very minute! If I strike you now, I'm afraid I'd kill you! You are sick, Rena Mae!" Ma Sybil scolded. After that Rena Mae washed the dishes under Zenna's supervision.

Ma Sybil said that something was desperately wrong with Rena Mae. Psychoanalysis was unheard of in the black ghetto during The Depression. The only behavior that warranted analysis was when someone ripped off their clothes, refused to eat, to talk, sat and stared into space, or ran into the streets nude. When any of those things happened, it was immediate cause to be sent to a mental institution for evaluation. Of course, Rena

Mae hadn't reached that point, but Ma Sybil wondered how soon it would be before she did. Ma Sybil also didn't have the money for therapy for Rena Mae's peculiar behavior. It took all she earned to keep her family and her body and soul together. Rena Mae had to find a way to keep in tune with the rest of the family.

A storm was brewing. Black clouds grew and ascended the sky. Their outline changed as Ma Sybil and Edna watched from the window. The restless breeze shivered in the dark trees. In the apex, the thunder muttered faintly and angrily all by itself. There were birds flying about the chimney of houses. Suddenly, the doorbell rang. Although Ma Sybil and Edna were good Christians, Edna was one of Yamacraw's leading Bolita runners and Ma Sybil played with her every playing day.

Many of the church members wouldn't place a bet with the local hustler at the candy store or grocery store. But over a cup of coffee or tea in their homes, they chimed and grinned as they recounted all the scandal in the neighborhood; and after all the chitchat, they made their bets with Edna.

Ma Sybil was a good Christian, but she didn't trust white people. She warned Rufus against fraternizing with people who was dirty in mind and attire. "A person may be poor and tattered, but there wasn't any reason on earth why a person should be filthy in body or mind." Ma Sybil often reminded him. "Soap and water wasn't that expensive and you certainly could think positively." Ma Sybil had always embedded that in the minds of children.

"Most of all, Rufus," Ma Sybil warned. "You mustn't trust white folks. Watch out for them at all times. They're apt to stab you in the back. It's hard enough for black women, but for black men, it is worst. White people will mutilate and lynch you. Just stay away from them. When you work for them, mind your business; be polite to them, but don't trust them."

This information confused Rufus even the more, but he supposed that Ma Sybil knew what she was talking about. She always did. But the information didn't help Rufus' baffled mind. It'll never be known for sure whether Rufus' emotional instability sprang from heredity or environment. Surely, there were enough factors in both branches to account for his temperament.

Ma Sybil and Edna made appetizing Homebrew, including blackberry wine and apple cider. Good corn liquor was always on hand, but they didn't make it. It was bought from suppliers. Not just anyone could walk into Ma Sybil's house and buy a drink. They had to be one of her church members or some of the dockworkers. When someone came to the door, Ma Sybil put down her sewing and strode to the door. She was regularly bargaining for her family. "How much?" Ma Sybil would ask, arranging her glasses on her eyes. She stumbled against the door jam, while still fumbling into her apron for the money. The vendor told her the price. "I can't pay that much," she shouted, pointing to the small army of children crowding around her each one hoping to get a blackberry or anything edible.

"All of them?" The solicitor asked. Ma Sybil nodded her head. "They are motherless and fatherless too." Still counting her coins over and over while watching the man's reaction from

under her glasses. "I'm the grandmother and their sole support."
Barley audible she spoke. "I can't spare a penny more." The
country bumpkin had compassion for her plight and gave in to
her price.

The eight-bedroom house wasn't enough. After Ma Sybil
brought the children home with her, she let two boarders go. Rufus
had his own room while Zenna and Rena Mae shared a room.
Lulu had a small bed in Ma Sybil's room. Ma Sybil still had two
boarders, and the rest of the house was left vacant when family
or friends visited.

When Rufus was fourteen, he worked at various jobs after
school. At sixteen, he dropped out. School didn't have
anything for him. Rufus convinced Ma Sybil, that their assets
would be more promising if he had a regular job. Rufus had an
offer as an apprentice barber in the neighborhood. He was good
at cutting hair. He had trimmed his two sister's hair and some of
the other children in the neighborhood as well. Zenna refused to
cut her tresses, she gloried her hair. Ma Sybil stated a woman's

hair was her glory and don't let anyone take your glory away.

3

CHAPTER THREE

Rufus was tidying up his chair in the barbershop. He glanced up and saw a radiant creature, his first customer for that day. She was about twenty-one with a wasp-like figure. Her thick, black hair was parted down the middle, revealing a pale scalp that resembled an over-ripe watermelon that was cracked by the sun. Her rich complexion was a Titan painting. She had raven eyes, coral lips, a high forehead, and large sparkling earrings hanging loosely from her ears. Her form was enveloped in beige attire and her dainty feet were encased in beige leather slippers. When she spoke, it was an affluent mezzo-soprano. You could see that she had American-Indian blood running through her veins. She marched over to Rufus' chair, plopped down, and crossed her long legs. Rufus eyed them cagily.

"Hi." She spoke softly and smiled faintly. "A trim please. Take some off the top and freshen up the V in the back. My name is Margie Gamble. What's yours?" Margie bent forward a little as Rufus put the mantel around her and snapped the safety pin.

"Hi." Rufus said with a boyish, sheepish grin. He told her his name and then started clipping her hair.

"Do you have a girlfriend?" Margie flirted.

"No!" Rufus answered emphatically. "I'm too young for that. I'm just sixteen. And besides, Ma Sybil would kill me if I had a girl."

"Ma Sybil?" Margie questioned. "And who's Ma Sybil?" She paused. Rufus helped her out of the chair.

"Ma Sybil's my grandmother," he stated. "She is taking care of me and my three sisters. Our parents are dead. Ma Sybil is very strict."

"I thought you were at least eighteen. Do you tell Ma Sybil everything?"

"No." Rufus answered slowly. "But I don't know anything about girls. Only what I've heard."

"How about me teaching you?" Margie laughed in a conventional way. "You must learn sometime."

"Yes, I know!" Rufus answered embarrassed.

"Think it over." Margie continued. "There isn't any rush. I'll be around and I'm sure you will also. But I'll tell you what you can do for starters. I have a flat, and I sell things." Margie paused and pouted her small dainty mouth. "I make and sell Homebrew."

Rufus knew all about Homebrew; Ma Sybil made excellent Homebrew. But she sold it to friends and church members, only. No one from the streets could walk in and buy Ma Sybil's drinks.

"I also sell corn-liquor. I don't make that though," Margie continued. "I rent rooms too. Should you know of anyone who wants a room for a while," Margie pivoted her weight from one leg to the other. "A real good time is going on at my place everyday, but Saturday night, it's a blast! Rufus, you must come some night. I don't run a rough place, but sometimes a person drinks too much. So, I need someone to encourage them to leave a little faster."

Madams of ill repute and ladies of the evening frequented the barbershop where Rufus worked. The women's neat appearance and their beauty were very important to them. Evening in Paris perfume lit up the barbershop and caused the skin to tingle with ecstasy. Before Rufus started working in the shop he didn't think that he would ever love a girl. The girls he knew always smelled so strong.

The girls who didn't smell pretty weren't attractive, with their long ashy legs and bare feet, and their clothes never fit right. Rufus' mother, Ma Sybil, and his sisters never reeked and surely they weren't unkempt. Ma Sybil's aroma was like ginger-cake and you could cuddle-up to her all day. Rufus could not tolerate a woman smelling strong. Once when he sang in the church choir, he gave it up and became an usher. "Rufus, you have a wonderful voice. Why did you give up singing in the choir?" Ma Sybil asked. "One Sunday, I had a sick spell from the scent of a girl's armpits and had to go to the recovery room," he stated.

"Why didn't you tell me about it?" Ma Sybil asked.

"Oh! She was a girl and I didn't want to make a fuss." Rufus answered.

Margie fluttered her naturally, curled long eyelashes. "Percy helps me out, but he is so old; thirty-five, at least. And he is a little too slow. It takes him forever to get them out, when one is disorderly. I think you'd make a better bouncer." Margie continued chatting away. "Every person that you send to my place, I'll tip you a dollar. I don't have a crowd but I would like too." Margie produced a small, pink sheet of stationary with her name on it.

"I must talk to my grandmother." Rufus said blushing at the bold statement coming from such a beautiful girl. "I must give account of my whereabouts." Rufus spoke softly and wondered what it would be like to be with a girl. "Ma Sybil could use the money. I have three younger sisters at home. I must explain where the extra money is coming from," he said to himself.

"You can always say that you're working a few hours at the produce market. They stay open all night." Margie gave Rufus a crooked smile. "It's strictly up to you how you handle it. Just don't tell her about us".

"Well now, I'm not that stupid." Rufus stated as he stared at Margie sidewise. Since Margie had invited Rufus to her flat, she was continuously in his thoughts. At times, he seethed in the imagination of kissing her brazenly, but tenderly. He spoke to her in tepid and breathless terms, but when Rufus was alone with Margie, all words he had expressed within himself had flown away.

CHAPTER THREE

Margie's four-room flat was located on Mott Street, near West Broad Street. The weather-hammered framed building was a dollar per week, unfurnished. Margie's place was always clean and neat. Luck smiled on Margie, but it didn't for other people during The Depression.

The lights were on when Margie rented the flat. The former occupant hadn't disconnected the wires in the box. A man whom called himself 'Free Light Man' would come around and connect Margie's lights for two dollars. During the day, the wires were disconnected, in case the meter-reader came along. But at night, the place was lit up like Las Vegas.

Margie's apartment was situated partly over the Chinese Restaurant, which was on Broad Street near the CCC office, which was also located on Mott Street. Margie's entrance was on Mott Street and so was Bessie Murtough's flat. But hers was opposite from Margie's. Bosom Bessie, that's what most people called her. Bessie had ten well-furnished rooms that she shared with her Chinese boyfriend, who owned the restaurant downstairs. Four pretty, young mulatto sisters from Augusta, Georgia also shared the flat. They were Bessie's live-in 'fille de joie'.

Bessie and her sister, Minnie Murtough, who lived across town, were the most flamboyant madams in Savannah. Years later, both sisters were chased out of town. It was known that many rich white men frequented Bessie and Minnie's dives. The secret had leaked to some of the wives concerning their husband's whereabouts; and the chase was on.

The stairs from the streets lead directly into Margie's living room. The living room was a Majestic Electronic photograph that played melodious music when a nickel was deposited. She also had a small table, some chairs and one window facing the living room door. The windows were heavily draped. The bedroom was at the left of the living room and contained a three-piece bedroom set. The room supplied ample light. A tiny kitchen lay to the right of the living room and displayed a small wood-burning stove. A small table and a half size window were also in the room. Just outside the kitchen door was a miniature hole in the wall. It was just large enough to enter into the precious bathroom. The bathroom housed a flush toilet with a chain that dangled from the tank. The ceiling, walls, and floor were planking. The floors were bare. There wasn't any heating system in Margie's apartment. The stove in the kitchen was sufficient to heat the entire flat. But, there wasn't any need for it, since the steam from the restaurant below kept the place comfortable during the winter, and like Dante's inferno in the summer.

On Saturday, the CCC, women workers collected their wages from the office downstairs. All day, people were busy up and down the stairs buying Margie's food and drinking Homebrew and Corn Liquor. The music box never stopped playing and some guests were in the bedroom making whoopee. Margie's flat was crammed the whole weekend. The common people seemed to identify with Margie's place instead of Bessie exquisite dive. Some of the customers went straight to Margie's after work. They were still wearing their work clothes when they entered Margie's door. Everything was down to earth. The music box, money collector made three trips on Saturday night to collect the money from the music box. The machine wouldn't play if it were full with nickels. Margie pocketed a quarter from every dollar. Bessie didn't have a music box, but she had her girls.

Monday morning, Margie was tired but her pockets were full with silver dust. Margie slept until noon on Mondays, then took a cab to the bank and deposited her money. Then she stopped for lunch. After President Roosevelt, closed banks, most black people were afraid to put their money into the bank. After the dissolution of the transaction, Margie shopped for clothes. She was a good businesswoman. She had ached for a man whom she could have a mutual understanding.

Margie detested pimps and women who allowed men to exploit them. She had high hopes that some day she would live like rich white folks. Margie's pith yearned for the finer entity. She wanted to be free from all the despotic men. Margie had a tough time at her father's stern hands in Marietta, Georgia.

CHAPTER THREE

Although, Margie thought that her father was a good dad, who protected his children, he was a miserable manager and husband. Margie's father drank heavily on weekends, chased women and beat her mother. Margie swore that what happened to her mother would never happen to her. She kept a buffer zone between herself and men. She decided that was the best way for her. Margie's parents agreed together how they were going to raise their children. The children couldn't alter favoritism from one parent or the other. In spite of the abuse Margie's mother suffered from her husband, she told them, "Love and respect your father. He is your father".

Respect! Yes Margie thought. But love hung somewhere in space. Margie could no longer stand to see her mother being mistreated by her father, and she left home. She had finished high school, but there wasn't any money for college. Margie left home before her eighteenth birthday.

During The Depression, speakeasies were everywhere in Savannah. That was how poor people lived. One Saturday night,

Rufus thought that he would visit Margie's flat. After the barber-shop was closed, he went home and gave Ma Sybil her share of the money. Rufus told Ma Sybil that he had a job at the produce market. Ma Sybil assured Rufus that it wasn't necessary to work around the clock; they were comfortable with what they had. Rufus persuaded Ma Sybil to let him try it out; and besides, he wanted new clothes. So Ma Sybil gave in. Rufus ate, washed, got dressed and headed for Margie's apartment.

When Rufus reached Margie's flat it was crazed with people. The music was blaring and folks were strutting all over the place, drinking and eating. Margie's grub was soon wiped-out and Rufus joined Percy in dispatching more food from the Chinese Restaurant downstairs. Rufus was thrilled with all the gaiety; he hadn't been in such a place before. All night the steps groaned with thumps of feet going up and down the stairs. Rufus was positioned as doorman. After peeping through a peephole he permitted the guests to come in.

CHAPTER THREE

An argument arose. "Hey man!" Rufus' voice hailed. "What are you doing lousing up the place?" Six feet, four, Percy marched over to the perpetrator and breezed down his neck.

"Yes, what are you doing?" Percy continued, "Lousing up the joint?"

Rufus and Percy quickly heaved the character out. After the guests had departed early Sunday Morning, Rufus again light-footed it downstairs to obtain breakfast for two. Margie washed-up and clad herself in a maroon, floor length, satin-stripe negligee with matching mules. When Margie opened the door, Rufus' eyes fell on this gorgeous creature. Rufus was flustered and baffled by all the glamour, and for a split second he wanted to run away. What was he going to do with that luscious, lively chick? He thought.

Rufus didn't even know how to talk to a woman who was so dazzling. He was afraid of his ignorance about sex and wondered whether he could please Margie, Of course not, he thought. His little worm, she probably couldn't feel it. What if he didn't please her? Margie might throw him out and he wouldn't even see her again. Rufus didn't want that to happened because he liked Margie so much.

Rufus liked everything about her; her mannerism, her moodiness, and he wanted to be around her. Rufus knew that he could learn so much from Margie, if he could satisfy her, he thought. How could he start making love to her and not seem juvenile and inexperienced. Rufus didn't know anything about a woman and sex, but mother nature and hormones always induced a way.

The scrawny, sweaty, smelly, plain girls that he knew turned him off. Rufus was friendly with the girls and talked to them, but never touched them. He had many erections and orgasms, but not from any of those girls. But from the first time he was around Margie, he was tormented by her looks and responses. Rufus didn't think he would ever like a girl enough to kiss and fondle until he met Margie.

CHAPTER THREE

After breakfast, Margie belched loudly, and excused herself for doing so, while wiping her mouth with a paper napkin. Margie stood up and gave Rufus a little peck on the head, as a reward. Rufus' knees became weakened and his ramrod was standing at attention.

"Finish!" Margie laughed in a high pitch. "I haven't even started with you yet!" Margie flung out her arms to Rufus. "Come." She said tenderly. Her deep dimples beckoned to Rufus. Margie pulled Rufus' head down to her and kissed him lightly and Rufus kissed her back. After they came up for air, Margie gave a deep sigh. "Please, fix two Moonshine drinks, Rufus." Margie always wanted to take some young man's innocence. The young man who had taken her chastity wasn't worldly at all. In fact, he was a little crude, under the circumstances.

Margie quickly swallowed the drink and eyed Rufus sipping his. Every sip Rufus shook his head like a chicken with the pip. "Undress. Take off every stitch." Margie spoke softly, her

59

big raven eyes caressing Rufus' firm, young, beautiful body. Rufus was beginning to feel the sensation from the booze. Once he had gotten into Margie's bed, she continued to instruct him. "Lie on your back," she said, smiling faintly. Margie became the aggressor; she seemed to be everywhere. Her tongue was like a butterfly wing across Rufus' face. Margie's firm young breasts pressed against Rufus' chest. Her black hair fell on his face. Margie made love to Rufus and he laid back powerless to do nothing more than accept her lovemaking. When it was over, Rufus went limp with pleasure and exhaustion. In the dim light, Rufus reached out and stroked Margie's hair.

"Margie, I'll never forget today." A wide smile mingled with glee flew onto Rufus' face. "It's the only time in my life that a girl ever made love to me. I enjoyed it very much. Now, it's my turn to make love to you. That's if you want me too." "Of course I want you too." Margie encouraged. Rufus fondled Margie's body, his courage had emerged and he entered her rhythmically. He wanted to please Margie and moved slowly and deeply. Margie clung to him, but Rufus sensed that she wasn't ready. He continued the steady rhythm for what seemed to him an eternity.

The pulse was beating against his temple and he was using all of his expertise to make them climax together. Rufus gritted his teeth and kept moving. Then he felt the unbearable, yet wonderful weakness flooded through his groins as they reached their climax together. Rufus fell down, exhausted and with the hope that he had satisfied her. Margie reached out and touched Rufus' cheek and she snuggled up against him and kissed him. "Rufus, you are a marvelous lover."

"Thanks!" Rufus uttered, wondering whether he was really a good lover or Margie was saying that to make him feel good. Rufus was pooped and when Margie dozed off and started to purr softly, he gently eased her out of his arms; got dressed hurriedly and crept dazzlingly downstairs. All the fresh assurance and gaiety had been left behind in the bedroom. Rufus was frightened about the new feelings.

After a number of Saturday nights out and Rufus advanced odor, mingled with exotic perfume, Ma Sybil knew what was going on. She had a talk with Rufus about growing up; which included women, disease, and pregnancy. Ma Sybil warned Rufus to be careful, and that Uncle Albert would talk to him about the man side of life.

Margie too was frightened about the new feelings that filled her with pleasure. And in her thoughts she went gropingly, cautiously, like Eliza in "Uncle Tom's Cabin," on the icy river.

Twilight was beginning. The wind ruffled the early autumn clouds, massing with the sky. They were deep purple shaded into an ashy lilac. Through the slip of the deluge of sunrise, beams poured in a yellow-yam color sprawling out like a giant fan. Action was always going on at Margie's place but not quite like on the weekend. During the week the regular theme was "Coon-can," but they played other games too. Margie extracted twenty-five cents out of every dollar. Just before the game was started, the theme was, "Take out the eights, nines, and tens." The women played as well as the men. Margie only played games for fun, not for money.

Within a year, after Rufus had met Margie, he was the best-dressed young man in Yamacraw. He had purchased two new suits, topcoat, raincoat, three pairs of new shiny shoes, four pairs of extra pants, six broad cloth shirts and two silk shirts. All smuggled in from China.

One morning, business wasn't proceeding at its regular pace, at the barbershop. Rufus went outside and sat on an apple crate and watched some men who were sitting on crates playing checkers. As Rufus watched, he also observed another group of disheveled vagabonds, with blood-shot eyes and drooling mouths. Some sat in doorways across the street. Others just sat on the ground with their backs pressed against the building, staring into space. They were old hustlers, tired, hungry, thirsty, disgusted, and smelling of death. Rufus was thrown with the dredge of humanity not a very good influence for an impressible, sensitive boy. And it took strength of character to rise above such degrading, hardened impact at that age. But it was the gateway into his new world.

One tramp approached the group of old hustlers. He was very hungry and thirsty. "How can I get a quick quarter? I'm hungry! Real hungry man!" The lone beggar whispered to himself. When the bum was paroled to the clump of vagrants, he stopped. "Hey man! Do you have anything to drink?" The lone rover asked while shuffling his feet.

"No!" They replied in unison. "We wish we did. We'd like to have a taste ourselves."

"Well, I'm going to stir up something." The lone drifter spoke as he stomped his foot nervously on the ground. "Shit man! I need something. I'll be back." The lone vagabond was trying to impress the gang that he was a good hustler.

As the lone plod shuffled off, a mass of air rushed through his guts playing the Grand Canyon Suite, almost uprooting him from the ground. "How can I get a good feed?" He asked himself. "I'll think of something," he stated. "I could snitch some fruit and run, he thought. Hell no! I want some real food." The drifter continued to walk and talk to himself. "Before The Depression, when I was hungry I could just walk into a cook-shop, and order whatever I wanted, and eat until my belly was full. Then I would tell the boss that I don't have any money to pay for the food. The boss would make you wash as many dishes as he wanted you to wash. But no more, because the son of a bitch boss, will call the dick, and they'll beat the shit out of you. Sometimes, the cops will lock your ass up."

"Well, the judge will guide you three days in the police. And all you get to eat while in jail is cornbread and black-eyed peas. And Oh Boy! Those damn chinches will eat your nuts up, too. I want some real food. I'll think of something," the derelict muttered as he went.

At that precise moment, the pauper's eyes picked up a pint jar lying in the gutter. He walked over to the bottle and nudged it with his foot. The flask was in one piece, and the former bourgeoisies had the common courtesy to cap the flask. The loafer picked up the bottle, opened it, and smelled where the delightful nectar had been.

The tramp threw his head back as far as he could and let the decanter rest on his tongue. A trickle graced his clapper. The lone tramp sighed and an idea came to him. With a jar in hand he marched to the nearest empty building. Once inside he emptied his bladder into the flask. He wiped the bottle off with his shirt-tail and then put the flask on the floor to cool down. When the bottle was room temperature, he grabbed the jar and emerged from building. When the drifter was in the midst of the tight-knit vagabonds, he offered them the flask. "Hey fellows, look!" The lone tramp whipped out the phial and held it up. "I have something here!" The bum spoke in a guttural tone. The group's eyes took on a sparkling glow at the sight of the golden corn-liquor, they thought. "One quarter!" The vagabond with rotted front teeth smiled, displaying his prize. "Fellows! You pay more than that from the dive. And this one hundred and fifty proof," the lone man spoke.

CHAPTER THREE

The sneaky-peters bowed their heads in agreement and started digging into their pockets for the necessary funds. They each pulled a penny here, three cents there, a nickel: until finally the required capital was obtained. They transferred the change to the merchant. When all the resources were politely itemized by the salesman, and from the anxious look on the other vagrant's faces, seemed as though it took forever to enumerate.

When the lone tramp was satisfied that every penny had been accounted for, he handed over the flask to the out-stretched hands and briskly walked away. "Have a good time, now. I got to split!" The departing swindler yelled over his shoulder. The air was calm as if it was tatted to the apex. A faint smile mingled with glee flew on all faces of the assembled clump of bums. The holder of the bottle gave a deep sigh and looked at the decanter and drew in a sharp breath between his teeth. Then with trembling hands he uncapped the flagon. The perpetrator had capped the jar as tight as he could to allow himself a few meters to split. When the flask was at last opened, the man held the bottle up and guzzled from it. After a swig, he spat out its contents. "Piss! Piss!" He shouted as he flung the flagon to the ground and watched the tinged liquid trickle out of the bottle. He coughed and hiccoughed, in a harsh sound. He wiped his mouth, bit his lip and for a second his eyes grew sad. Some of the cronies tottered in the direction of the swindler, but he had disappeared around the corner forever.

"You son of a bitch! You cock sucker! You bastard! You mammy rider!" The group called out, stomping their feet and flailing their arms into the air. Then, one very disappointed fellow piped in. "If I ever see you again, I'll put my foot up your very ass hole!"

The vagabonds lashed every epithet at the scoundrel that was in their intellect. When they had exhausted themselves, they quietly assembled again, with sorryful eyes and parched throats. They eyed each other shyly. Then, one homeless man picked up a cigarette butt from the ground and lit it. He puffed greedily on the butt and then gave out a belly laugh. "Give it to the son of a bitch." He puffed again. "That Joe sure did take us. And we are old hustlers." The whole group chuckled loudly. They coughed, farted, and spat on the ground until they were too exhausted to do anymore. "Let that be a lesson to all." Another vagrant advised the bunch. "Taste before you pay."

There were some hard days during The Depression. Rufus watched the vagabonds. Their drained out feeble bodies and their disoriented minds made Rufus swear their fate would never happen to him, ever. And as soon as he could leave Yamacraw, he'd do so. But he wasn't going to leave Yamacraw as long as Ma Sybil was alive. Was that all it was to life? Rufus thought. No wonder his mother committed suicide. "Rufus, a customer!" His boss diverted Rufus' attention from the homeless men.

A tall, stout, dark skinned man sat down in Rufus' chair. Rufus smiled faintly and bowed his head gently, while he placed the mantel around the man's neck. "What'll you have?" Rufus asked the serious looking man, who looked to be between forty-five and fifty years old. "A light trim." The man answered, as he brushed off imaginary particles from his well worn, navy blue pants. His clean white starched shirt collar was somewhat frayed. The man's thick, black, tough hair dotted with gray stood out at Rufus. Rufus glanced down at his mirror polished flourished shoes. He must be a pimp, Rufus thought, as he began clipping the man's hair.

"How goes everything, Big Luke?" The owner asked.

"Oh, so, so." Big Luke replied, who still seemed to be locked deep in thought. After the job was completed, Big Luke paid his bill and tipped Rufus ten cents. Big Luke left without uttering another word.

"Rufus! Do you know who he was?" The Boss asked.

"No. You called him Big Luke," Rufus stated. "Seems like I've heard the name though, but I just can't place it".

"Well, you were too young to know about Big Luke when he was in full swing." The boss said. "Luke isn't from Yamacraw. He was born in west Savannah to well off parents.

CHAPTER THREE

They owned their home. Luke's father was a preacher and his mother a midwife.

Luke needed one year to finish high school, but he dropped out. There was no persuading him to go back.

"Just one year to finish?" Rufus spoke. "He should've completed that, and he could've preached or been a male-nurse."

"None of that stuff for Big Luke," the barber continued, smiling faintly. "Luke relished a different kind of life. I heard that Luke's parents were very strict with him, when he was young. He resented that. Luke purposely did a lot of things to get back at his parents."

"Well, that's the way some families are." Rufus stated. "Every person is an individual you know! And much as one likes to change a person, it just can't be done."

"Yes, people are becoming aware of that now." The boss replied. Luke Swaine was an Atlas looking man, a real lethargic. He once lived a towering life around town. Luke never married, he just shacked-up with different women. At times, he lived alone in hotels or in high-class rooming houses. When Luke was down on his luck, he stayed at home with his parents. He never held a job. He was a real hustler. His profession was mugging, gambling, numbers running, picking-pockets, and breaking into houses. And for sweet meat, he raped black women and released them of their funds. Luke was a real sex maniac. His physical apparatus was his compass, but the needle didn't swing above his neck.

A storm was brewing. Black clouds grew and ascended the sky. Their line changed as one watched from the window. The restless breeze shivered in the dark trees. In the apex the thunder muttered faintly and angrily all by itself. In the late 20's, there were a series of rape/muggings in Savannah, Georgia. In the early 30's, the act excelled. A black man preyed on black domestic women on their way home, especially on payday.

Luke would stakeout his victims and attacked them in an alley, lane, or some remote area. He never physically hurt any of the women. Law enforcement were on the lookout for the perpetrator. But since the incidents concerned all blacks, they didn't put too much emphasis on the subject. One night, Big Luke's prey was a tall, buxom, ginger-colored woman in her 30's. Luke stepped from behind a tree with a pistol and pointed at the woman's head. He directed her into an empty garage door. "Just do as I say and you won't get hurt."

"Oh, you don't have to hold a gun on me." The woman said nervously. "I'm a woman and I can't beat you anyway. I'll do anything that you say. Please don't hurt me? I have an eight year old son to support."

"Now, you're a sensible woman". Luke spoke boldly. "Give me all your money. Give me the pan. Food for your son, huh?"

"Yes sir." Clara Ward said, giving up the money and the pan. "My son is waiting for me. I'm a widow. I don't have a boyfriend," Clara encouraged.

After Luke had collected the money and searched the pan, he lowered his guard. Feeling vain and proud of himself for stirring the woman's imagination: he pocketed the money and the gun. "Lay down!" Luke demanded, as he placed the purse and pan on the floor. Clara fell to the ground. She pulled up her pleated flapper skirt, with a wide belt and a big bow on the left side. Dry leaves were scattered over the garage's floor. Since Clara hadn't had sexual action for some time, she was almost a virgin. Luke's huge arrow had trouble penetrating the target. Clara took her cue and feigned anxiety. "Let me fix it!" Clara spoke hastily.

"Okay!" Big Luke snapped. "Make it snappy!" Clara found a straight razor she was carrying, hidden in a pocket in her petticoat. She fumbled with the big pole with on hand. "I'll need some spit," Clara informed Luke. "Raise up a little".

"All right!" Luke uttered sharply. "Hurry up! Damn it!" Clara spat a huge glob of saliva into her hand.

"Raise up a bit." Clara said gently the second time. Luke complied with Clara's request. Clara massaged his large meat with her hand and she held it firmly over her vulva, touching it quickly. With the other hand, she made a strong sweeping motion and with all her power, she swung the razor on the part where Luke's conceit was stored. Clara detached the stretched out, crane neck object.

"What in Hell is you doing?" Luke exclaimed, jumping up and almost tripping on his pants. Luke now realized what had happen to him. The gun fell to the floor in the darkness. Luke, in excruciating pain, didn't look for the gun. "You dirty bitch! I'll get you for this!" Luke wailed as he galloped down Tutti-Frutti Lane.

"I got him!" Clara's mezzo-soprano voice sounded, as she dashed into the first door that was opened. Windows and doors were now being opened and voices inquiring, "What was that?" The questions were heard all around.

"The mugger! I got him!" Clara said, displaying the short piece of muscles in one hand and the razor in the other. Every one fell back.

"What's going on here?" Inquired a white male, as he approached the group.

"The mugger! The rapist!" Clara gasped for breath, still exhibiting her treasure. "I got him! Call the police? I just cut off the attacker's dick. He robbed me and was in the process of raping me. But I got him! He won't get fat without this!"

Finally, the puzzle began to fall into place. Someone had already called the police. Luke Swaine had hobbled into the first emergency hospital entrance that he saw. Soon it was known all over town about the missing penis. Clara related the whole story to the police and they found the gun.

"Well, when he gets out of the chain gang." One policeman said. "I wonder what he'll work with." They chuckled. "He still has his tongue and fingers," cited another. "Yes, that isn't the same thing. I sure wouldn't like that to happen to me."

Luke Swaine was sentenced to five years on the Georgia chain gang. After two years out of circulation, he was once again on the turf. For a while, Luke directed his activities to gambling and other ornate acts. But no muggings or robberies were ever committed by a man of Luke's description. After his jail stretch, he no longer smiled and joked with the guys. Nor did he brag about his conquests among his fellow conspirators. Now, Luke in his 50's, was stout and very remorseful looking.

For months, women went about their duties without fear of being molested. Then, suddenly Luke Swaine's name was on people's lips again. Luke met a beautiful, young lady and began to date her. The woman didn't know about his past. In the process of lovemaking, Luke broke a large piece of bologna sausage off into the woman's vagina. The sausage was so embedded that it had to be removed by a doctor. Luke was again incarcerated, and had to serve out his former sentence, plus one year for recent delirium. When Luke had served his time, he was again on the streets. An underground newspaper printed flyers about Luke and his satanic endeavors, with his photo blown up.

It wasn't known for sure, what press, black or white displayed Big Luke so elegantly to the public. The copies acquainted most of the black women with Luke Swaine, and they eyed him cautiously. Rufus never knew whether Luke went straight or not. But, one thing was for sure, he didn't want to identify any of the people he had seen that day.

At church, one bright Sunday in April, the parishioners shook hands and greeted on another after service. "Rena Mae! You're growing up." A member of the congregation congratulated. "How pretty you look today." Another member exclaimed. Rufus', five-seven, olive-skinned, second sister was the most comely and the lightest complexion of all the children, blushed. "The pink chambray dress fits you to the tee, Rena Mae! You've grown to be a beautiful young lady. Now, you look exactly like your mother." Another member said. Rena Mae smiled, her head held high like a swan among a flock of geese.

Ma Sybil had brought the material at five cents a yard from Yachum and Yachum's, fire sale. After a good washing, all of the dark stains were removed. Zenna and Ma Sybil had designed and fitted the garment into a lovely outfit. And the dress brought out Rena's full potentials.

Through the clean window pane of the house, miniature dust particles danced in horizontal beams that streamed through a spring day in Yamacraw. The early Crocuses, Tulips, Daffodils, and Narcissuses, snipped by birds, were completely matured and scattered sperm over the earth. Rena Mae was so proud of her new outfit, so much so, that when Ma Sybil asked who would go to the drugstore for her, Rena Mae volunteered. That wasn't something Rena Mae was known to do. Rena Mae, fifteen, matured early, like a Georgia peach. Rena Mae's pink dress had a wide sash from the same material, which pointed out her petite waist. Her girlish, angular figure, smarted an innocent mixture of adolescence and flowering youth. Rena Mae's swollen breasts weighted noticeably against her dress. Her Pocahontas face, large brown eyes sparkled, bashfully and mischievously. Her curly hair brushed out into a pageboy, caused heads to turn. She pranced down the street as if an audience were watching her antics. Rena Mae's starched, flared skirt ruffled in the wind and she glanced into the plate glass window to see the effect. When Rena Mae strode into the drugstore, the air instantly became charged with her force of vitality. There was something about Rena Mae that was set apart from her sisters.

"Gee! You look pretty!" Frank's tone was so obviously admiring that Rena Mae merely said, "Thank you." Frank, the drug store delivery boy was a white, drop out and his pale face lit up when Rena Mae merely said thank you. Frank would have been almost handsome, if he wasn't so thin. His razor sharp collarbone glistened beneath the old green, faded polo shirt he was wearing. The drugstore owner had many delivery boys in the past, but Frank, who lived with a large family on Oglethrope Street, had stayed longer than the rest. Frank, fifteen, the same age as Rena Mae, had winked slowly and elaborately at her contorting one side of his face.

"Rena Mae was always so clean, pretty, and neatly pulled together," Frank thought. "Hell! That nigger gal's clothes is cleaner and nicer than my sister's. I'd sure like to get some of that," he thought smiling. While Rena Mae was waiting for the prescription to be filled for Ma Sybil's arthritis, she browsed around the store until she hooked a Baby Ruth candy bar and dropped it into her bag. Frank, dusting and arranging the shelves, was still admiring Rena Mae's body, when he saw her drop the candy bar into her pocketbook. Suddenly, Frank was called to deliver some packages; of course, he wouldn't tell on Rena Mae. He was poor also, and poor people have something of a spirit for one another. They are perforce, bound together in comradeship of a sort in that close atmosphere, he thought. Wasn't his boss rich? He owned the big drugstore, a car, and a plush home on Victory Drive. What's a candy bar?

Frank was his parents' oldest child. His father was unemployed for a long time, but now he had a steady job with the CCC. He was boss over a group of old black women who cleared vacant lots in the city. Frank hopped onto his rickety bike, which squeaked as he went to make his deliveries.

Frank's mind raced thinking of Rena Mae. He had admired her but today her delight propelled him. Frank had winked at Rena Mae sometime ago; at first, she wasn't sure that her had winked or if something was in his eye. But that day he made it certain. Frank had blown Rena Mae a wink and she caught it with a gesture that was juvenile and carnal.

When Frank was parallel to Rena Mae, he said. "You love Baby Ruth candy, huh?" He smiled faintly, showing his perfect rat like teeth. Frank's head heaped with read hair, turned like a snakes head, in all directions. Rena Mae was frightened, but she had no intention of admitting her crime. She smiled cagily, but did not answer.

"I love Baby Ruth, too." Frank's smile broadened as he produced two bars of the same candy and handed them to her. They both giggled. Rena Mae hissing through her clinched teeth, as was her way, when she laughed. Frank bit into a Baby Ruth, as he cocked his red, wavy adolescent head.

"I'd like to see you sometimes. I can give you all the candy you can eat. But you must promise not to tell." Frank told her. Rena Mae eyed the oil and small beads of sweat on his noise slinking among freckles.

"I won't tell". Rena Mae spoke for the first time, and looked at Frank inquiringly. "See you where?" She said smiling and fidgeting with the paper bag. "You can't see me in the neighborhood either, everybody knows us. And my younger sister follows me everywhere".

"Well, she isn't with you now." Frank said, catching the point of coquetry she had thrown.

"That's because she's doing her homework." Rena Mae switched off, suddenly becoming conscious of her body as a young woman. From that moment her childhood period was over.

Rena Ma's beauty was as structural, as a Georgia Pine. The only thing that could damage it was an accident, disease, or old age. One day, Rena Ma and Lulu strolled into the drugstore to purchase medication for Ma Sybil. A note changed hands. The note stated that Frank was leaving the drugstore for a better pay-ing job near his home. Maybe, we can still get together sometimes, he wrote. Frank was tremendously developed for his age, and he was very friendly with the black boys who hung around the drugstore.

One day, out back of the drugstore a group of boys went to the high weeds to pee. Frank on his break joined them. "Man what a cock you got!" One of the black boys stated, eyeing the phenomenon. Frank giggled, he was proud of his large penis. The white girls whom he had sex with, said that Frank's dick was like a nigger's pecker. "It takes something like this to satisfy the women." Frank smiled further, shaking the piss off his prick and returning it to his pants. Another lad still held his penis out. "Mine's big too see!" Displaying his ware all around so that the gang could see what he had.

"Pshaw! Shit man!" Another spoke up. "Your little worm beside that donkey's dick is like father and son," they chuckled.

"I wonder how it got so big?" One boy exclaimed, after Frank had gone back into the store.

"Fucking! Fucking man! How else?" Stated another, as he humped a few times demonstrating.

"But, where did he get all that pussy, at his age?" stated another, amazed.

"Who knows?" A boy answered. "Could be older women. You know that he has lots of sisters." They snickered.

"Man that diamond cat got a piece of meat on him." Spoke one of the group, detaching a weed from its stem. "Shoot! Frank's dick is bigger than any spade cat I've seen. Man, Frank has a hammer like David," said another. "Who is David?" One guy, who knew nothing about the arts, asked. They were stilled amazed about the episode. They playfully pissed some more and two boys let the steam of piss crisscross as two swords in fencing. They giggled and scattered.

Rena Mae was frightened because she had eaten so much of Frank's candies and hadn't given him anything in return. The thought of it, upset her so much, she thought the KKK would come and take them out and lynch them. Every time the doorbell rang, fear gripped Rena Mae. The mob, she thought. "Lord! I have done it now!" But she didn't know what she had done.

That night, the thought of the KKK, disturbed Rena Mae so that she slept rocky. Rena Mae had a nightmare. She dreamed she was lying flat on her back, on a bench under the Chinaberry tree in the back yard taking a nap. A towering, gigantic, Adonis, Chestnut horse, ambled into the back yard; his big prick extended. She tried to escape but had no chance. Rena Mae cried out alarmingly. But no one heard or saw them, even though people were passing right by the fence. The stud straddled the bench over Rena Mae. He dropped his weight pendulum into her vagina, tearing right through her dress, slip, panties, and penetrating her sex like an arrow. It was so painful that Rena Mae cried out loud with all her might; but still, no one heard her. Rena Mae was fully coherent when she felt Zenna, poking her in the ribs. "Rena Mae! Wake up! You're having a nightmare!"

CHAPTER THREE

Rena Mae, laboriously opened her eyes, she was wet with perspiration and trembling uncontrollably. Rena Mae was so tired, the incubus had upset her so much, she had completely forgotten about the KKK. After Rena Mae's nerves were calmed, sleep crept into her soul. She awoke in the morning to the tune of Ma Sybil rattling the lid on the stove. Rena Mae felt safe again and she put the lynch-mob out of her mind, forever.

4

CHAPTER FOUR

After Frank left the drug store, Jim Nelson, a black boy
was hired. Although Frank and Rena Mae's relationship never
blossomed: Jim, who was also intrigued by Rena Mae, had better
luck. Jim and Rena Mae soon had secret relations going on.
When Rena Mae returned to school in September, she was pregnant from Jim. She began to blossom. Ma Sybil noticed in her
appearance that which spelled only one thing. How could that
be? Ma Sybil thought. She wasn't slack with the girls, and she
checked them every month, and everything was all right. Ma
Sybil just couldn't understand how such a thing could happen to
Rena Mae. If what she was thinking was true. But something

was wrong with Rena Mae, and Ma Sybil was going to get to the bottom of it.

Ma Sybil knew that Rena Mae was sly, foul mouthed, and wasn't above a little frog-caking. She was capable of many things, but how could she pull this off. Ma Sybil was puzzled. Ma Sybil was a clever woman also. Locked in a room, she sat Rena Ma on a chair and stared her in the eyes. Ma Sybil questioned Rena Mae about the deceit. She admitted that she had sex with Jim Nelson. And when she told him that she was a few days late, he supplied her with mercurochorome each month. Ma Sybil was outraged about the deception, and she stormed about the room upbraiding Rena Mae.

"Rufus! Don't you think we should knock on the door and ask mercy for Rena Mae?" Zenna asked with misty eyes.

"No!" Rufus shook his head. "Ma Sybil knows what she is doing," Rufus assured Zenna blandly. "Anyway, Rena Mae had it coming, always so fresh and uppity." Zenna took the insults in silence.

Rufus didn't have any sympathy for Rena Mae. She had broken his first fountain pen and he'd flung a lump of mud at her. Ma Sybil and Zenna had brought Rufus the gift for his thirteenth birthday. No one in Yamacraw had a pen like that. When the pen was filled with ink you could write for a long time. Rena Mae took the pen from Rufus' room and carried it to school. She showed it around and gave it to a boy.

Ma Sybil insisted that Rena Mae get the pen back, but the pen was never right. The ink would gush out at times and ruin the documents. Rufus had choked Rena Mae until Zenna pulled him off of her. He was angry. Maybe, that 's the same boy who messed her up, he thought,

When the door opened Ma Sybil and Rena Mae emerged, looking tired. "I have found out what I wanted to know," Ma Sybil stated as she dabbed at her eyes trying to stem the flow of tears. "Rena Mae has done a terrible injustice to herself and her family. She has deceived us." Rufus and Zenna stood transfixed while Ma Sybil sobbed uncontrollably; they tried to comfort Ma Sybil.

"What's wrong with Rena Mae, Ma Sybil?" Zenna questioned.

"Rena Mae is pregnant!" Ma Sybil commented. "I tried to do my best. I warned you girls; if anyone disgraced this house they'd have to leave. You must be ladies. Rena Mae, don't have to leave tonight, but first thing in the morning. So start packing now."

Ma Sybil strode to the kitchen and lifted the cover off the pot roast with one hand and dabbed at her eyes with the other. "I'm an old woman. I've raised my children and I'm trying to bring up my daughter's children. I have no intention of getting involved with a third generation." Ma Sybil sauntered back and forth unconsciously, opening and closing cabinet doors. Taking one food from the pantry to discover it wasn't the food she planned to use, and placing it back into the wrong bin. "Rena Mae is woman enough to make a baby; she must have the responsibility of that child and herself. She may visit us any time, and if she gets hungry, come home to eat. Rena Mae needs her own place." Ma Sybil stopped talking, and the case was closed. Rena Mae was too proud, and she had no intention to come crawling back for anything.

"I'll show them." Rena Mae, thought to herself, as she sulked and cried.

"Oh, goody!" Lulu's girlish thin voice flowed indistinctly through the kitchen door. "Now I can have a bed all by myself." Ma Sybil's eyes bored a hole into Lulu's eyes and she didn't pursue the matter. Although, Lulu adored Rena Mae, at times, she tried to imitate Rena Mae in many ways. But she didn't like Rena Mae causing Ma Sybil to weep. For that she hated her. And Lulu remembered Rena Mae had struck her on the head many times when she tried to follow her someplace. Zenna the emotional one in the family dashed into the bathroom and locked the door. Rufus nonchalantly strode over to the kitchen sink and picked up a paring knife and began pealing potatoes; while Ma Sybil scraped the carrots for the pot-roast that was bubbling for their dinner.

When Rena Mae awoke the next morning, she felt as if she had emerged from under twenty feet of water. She took her battered suitcase that was left over from her parents. Through a shower of tears she left the house like a fugitive. She was so distraught that she didn't even say goodbye, and no one said goodbye to her. Everybody was hidden away some place wishing it were a bad dream.

The fresh morning air seemed to drive fear into Rena Mae. The birds singing and dew drenched trees appeared to be addressing her directly, mocking her. Ma Sybil threw her out! Ma Sybil threw her out! Rena Mae thought. Rena Mae staggered blindly along the streets with her weighted bag and mind. She headed for Uncle Albert's house who lived on Taylor and Jefferson Street. Uncle Albert lived in a black middle-class section that wasn't located in Yamacraw. Rena Mae struggled with her luggage and her thoughts. She hated all of them at home, and she wished that they all were dead; especially, Ma Sybil. "Why couldn't she let me stay? Ma Sybil never liked me anyway, always picking on me. Don't do that, Rena Mae! You're sitting with your legs too far apart. Close your legs dear! Little boys are looking," she thought. "I hate her! I hate her!" Rena Mae expressed out loud, as she sat on her luggage to rest.

If it had been Zenna she wouldn't have thrown her out." Rena Mae again expressed out loud. "Come, Zenna! Zenna is my adding machine." Rena Mae mimicked her grandmother, as she damned all of them in her heart.

Rufus heard Rena Mae when she crept out that morning. But after the fountain pen incident, Rufus was hurt and his softness toward Rena Mae had ebbed out. But that morning as he heard his sister leave, his mind wondered back to when they were children.

The soothing sun in October showed it had little power. The sky was light blue and there was threaded frigidness in the air. That was the first day that the children were allowed to keep their shoes on after school. The entire summer the children's feet were innocent of shoes. While Rufus sat on the swing on the front porch, he occasionally glanced at the children across the street. The groups of children were dashing up and down the steps, laughing and pushing. One girl stood sucking her thumb, waiting her turn to mount the stairs, her braids projecting from her head like arrows from a target. Another girl who waited her turn wore a soiled, tattered dress. The hem was ripped out on one side and hung down, giving her the effect of a bird with a broken wing. When it was Rena Mae's turn, her long skinny, pipe-stem legs dangling in over size, high-top, navy-blue sneakers. She looked like a dasher sticking up out of a milk churn. After a few jumps, suddenly Rena Mae's shoe sole, detached itself from the top and mushroomed all the way down the stairs.

A howl went up from the group and pervaded the air, as they pointed to Rena Mae's shoe. Rufus didn't want to laugh but a small bark escaped before he could stop it. Rena Mae didn't lay emphasis on the matter; she yanked the top off, discarded it and continued her play with just one shoe.

Rufus wondered how she would handle the situation at this point. In spite of all Rena Mae's mischief, tears welled up in Rufus' eyes. She was his sister and he loved all his sisters. Wasn't he the man of the house?

Zenna also heard Rena Mae leave, but she was so choked-up she kept her head covered and cried. Lulu was fast asleep and didn't hear anything. Ma Sybil heard Rena Mea leaving, but she too was affected about the whole situation, she kept still and prayed. "Lord! Go with the child. Please keep Rena Mae from all harm. Lord! Please direct that child," Ma Sybil cried.

Rena Mae rang Uncle Albert's doorbell. After she had entered, she explained everything to Uncle Albert and Aunt Callie. They eyed each other in bewilderment. Suddenly, Uncle Albert went over to Rena Mae and put his arms around her while she sobbed incoherently. "My own sister, Agnes', little skinny

Rena Mae, has grown-up," stated Uncle Albert. "Now, now, don't carry on so." Uncle Albert embraced her tightly. Aunt Callie strode over and began stroking Rena Mae's eyes covered in her own tears. "This isn't the end of the world, you know?" Uncle Albert continued. "Ma Sybil isn't young anymore, and she isn't well. This is a shock to her. I tell you what we'll do, I'm sure that I can speak for my wife." Aunt Callie bowed her head in agreement.

"We must leave for work soon, but you eat some breakfast, rest and get some sleep. We'll be home around four o'clock. When you get some rest, go out and find a room, leave your suitcase here. Be here when we return and we'll go with you and talk to your landlady; and pay her a month's rent. We'll pay your rent until the baby is a month old. In the meantime when you get hungry, food is always here." Uncle Albert spoke warmly.

Rena Mae found a large airy front room on the first floor, with cooking privileges. The room had a three-piece bedroom suit, a good condition linoleum covered floor, clean curtains hung at the window, a large fireplace, two chairs and a closet. The room was so close to the street if Rena Mae extended your arm she could touch the people passing by.

After dinner, Rena Mae showed Uncle Albert and Aunt Callie the room that she selected. The Room was a dollar a week, just a short distance from Uncle Albert's house. All were pleased with the room. Uncle Albert paid four weeks rent. The landlady was very pleased about that and showed it with a big smile exposing two missing, upper front teeth.

Rena Mae sat on the bed as tears coursed down her face. "Why are you crying? Aren't you pleased with the room?" Uncle Albert asked. "Yes, I'm pleased with the room, but I miss my family and home," Rena Mae expressed.

Uncle Albert strode over to Rena Mae, put his arms around her shoulders and said, "Please stop crying. I know you miss your family. But, you are not alone." Uncle Albert spoke, as he tilt Rena Mae's head up. He smiled and stood back with folded arms looking down at Rena Mae. "You were the smallest, reddest and most wrinkled baby I ever saw. Now, you're a beautifully, blossomed young woman and soon to be mother." Uncle Albert stated smiling broadly. That made Rena Mae giggle a bit and soon a cheerful smile crossed her face.

Jim had told his parents about Rena Mae's pregnancy, but they didn't want to hear about it. "Why doesn't she put the baby up for adoption?" Jim's mother stated. "You know how stressed we've been. For one year I was the only breadwinner in this family. You have a low paying job, and your dad hasn't made a pay check, yet. So you two must work it out." Jim's mother confirmed.

The mellow December sun came streaking into the room. The sky was light blue and there was cordial warmth in the air. It was Christmas Day. For sometime Rena Mae had inwardly nursed a steel spore implanted in her because she was evicted from her grandmothers home. But time healed the wound and the animosity was short lived. Rena Mae was reconciled with her family and went to visit them on Christmas Day. Rena Mae's beauty was enhanced and she managed to buy a new maternity dress and shoes. She also bought gifts for the entire family and a special gift for Ma Sybil, a beautiful silk scarf. Ma Sybil flinched inside, at the idea of how she got it. The family had presents for Rena Mae too. And she was graced with her regular place at the dinner table, and so were Uncle Albert and Aunt Callie.

They enjoyed the turkey dinner with all the trimmings. Rena Mae thought that Ma Sybil was the best cook in the world, and so did many other people who lived in Yamacraw. Rena Mae was gay and cheerful that day. She had missed them very much and they had missed her. Rena Mae had resigned herself to her situation. She had already made friends with a group of people who thought and acted like she did. After dinner, Rena Mae didn't tarry long. She had planned to stop by the drugstore where Jim Nelson worked. When Rena Mae had reached Broughton Street and West Broad, Mr. Monroe, a middle-aged man with a peg leg who had a pushcart was parked at the corner selling his wares. Mr. Monroe sold a variety of goods but his famous articles were roasted peanuts, cooked crabs, still hot from the burner, and candy bars.

Rena Mae had known Mr. Monroe most of her life. Every one in Yamacraw knew him. Mr. Monroe and Ma Sybil were small entrepreneurs. Mr. Monroe is working on Christmas Day! Why isn't he at home eating turkey dinner? She said to herself. His wife Sarah must be serving the white-folks today, and his she will bring him a plate when she comes home. Sarah, a good, kind, domestic, lived in an alley about five blocks from Ma Sybil. Mr. Monroe likes to play around with young girls and he tried to subdue them. He was a church person and since no report had been made against him, the validity of the situation was never brought forth.

Rena Mae's mind floated to the circumstance of the pass when she was twelve. She and two girl friends were headed home through the alley. When they were parallel to Mr. Monroe's house, he was standing in his doorway. "Hey, pretty girls!" He called out. "Come in! I have some candy for you." He stood fidgeting, his bucolic hand holding the candies. The girls had heard about the fresh old man, but they weren't afraid of him. They were three to his one, and besides he had only one leg. They went in. Mr. Monroe gave up the candy, and immediately tried to fondle Rena Mae. She promptly slapped his face and they dashed from the shack and ran out of the alley, giggling, and eating the candies.

"Come back pretty girls and give me a kiss!" Mr. Monroe yelled, as he hobbled out on the porch. "Come back! I'll give you a dollar!" He called to them. The girls were already out of the alley and the candies were devoured. Different neighbors had seen young girls coming and going into Mr. Monroe's house. But there wasn't a complaint and too, The Depression was in; and that had become the way of life.

When Rena Mae was fourteen, one day on her way home, Mr. Monroe and his pushcart were parked at the corner.

"Pretty girl have crab cake on me." Holding the succulent meat. Rena Mae didn't answer him or cut her stride. Mr. Monroe plopped after her. "I'll give you a dollar for a kiss." Rena Mae still said nothing. "If you come to my house, I'll give you two dollars." He continued to make advances. Rena Mae's patience exhausted turned and faced Mr. Monroe. "If you ever say any-thing to me again," she blasted. "I'll tell my grandmother and my brother. And my brother will kick your old gray ass." Mr. Monroe didn't approach the subject further. But he held a smo-thering resentment against Rena Mae.

After Christmas dinner at Ma Sybil's, Rena Mae saw Mr. Monroe and his pushcart. "Ah ha!" Mr. Monroe spoke walking behind Rena Mae after he saw her with the big stomach. He grinned and tried to get revenge. "You wouldn't have me!" He spoofed. "I wasn't good enough for you. Now look at you. I would've been careful. I wouldn't have knocked you up. And you don't have a husband nedder." Mr. Monroe chuckled as he plodded along behind Rena Mae, mocking her.

Rena Mae already stressed about her condition, strode over to Mr. Monroe, her eyes all flamed. "You old gray son of a bitch." She shouted as loud as her voice would carry. "I wouldn't shit in your mouth, much less in your hand. Go beat your old meat with your fist like you always do. You bastard!" Rena Mae used the most derogatory epithets to make the situation crystal clear to Mr. Monroe. "If you ever speak to me again, I'll have my man kick your old black ass, all over town!" Rena Mae stood glaring down at Mr. Monroe, his boundless dirty eyes drank her in, but he didn't speak. People stopped and starred. Mr. Monroe pushed his cart away, and when he thought he was at a safe distance he stopped. "My Lord! That girl got a tongue on her. I never heard such a mouth on a pretty young girl in all my life." Mr. Monroe finally smiled faintly, shook his old gray head slightly, and plopped down the street. Rena Mae had a maverick temper. She always spoke her mind without fear of favor.

CHAPTER FOUR

In April, Rena Mae gave birth to a girl without any trouble. Jim was at her side when the baby arrived. He named her Kay. After their stay in the hospital, Uncle Albert and Aunt Callie went to fetch them home. Rena Mae stood smiling holding tiny Kay in her arms. She strode to Aunt Callie and placed the baby into her arms. They smiled and Aunt Callie talked baby talk to Kay and then placed the baby into Uncle Albert's arms. Then they left for Rena Mae's room.

Kay was tiny, normal, healthy, and very wakeful. She cried most of the time. The constant wail for Kay upset Rena Mae so much that she began to cry too. No matter what Rena Mae did for her, after an hour or so the wailing started again. The doctors said that it was gas. "Was it because Kay recognized my lack of experience and uncertainty?" Rena Mae thought. Was she the clumsy, young mother who never did anything right? "I shouldn't had her," Rena Mae spoke out loud. "I'm not made to be a mother. I'm too young. Kay has such a slippery body. I'm afraid to bathe her. I might drop her." Rena Mae became so frustrated, she didn't know how to cope with the situation; so she just sponged Kay's tiny body.

The fresh May air was warm and saturated with spices. The birds sang in the glossy trees, droves of bees flew and buzzed around the pungent cardinal-red and shocking pink roses and other flowers in the yard. Rena Mae took Kay to Uncle Albert and Aunt Callie's house; their house would be the first she would visit.

Uncle Albert and Aunt Callie had been so kind and considerate to her. Somewhere lurked inside Rena Mae's mind that they would adopt Kay. Uncle and Aunt cuddled Kay, fed her, praised her, and went as far as pressing into Kay's tiny fist a five-dollar bill. But they didn't express any desire to adopt her.

Jim Nelson, the baby's father gave Rena Mae as much support as he could. He stopped by daily. The only bath that Kay got was when Jim bathed her. Jim had helped his sister with her children and knew how to handle babies. He was also proud that he could produce a living being. Rena Mae and Jim grinned and played, as they admired the product of their love.

Rena Mae dressed Kay in her new outfit. She looked like a little doll, so prim and pretty. She also dressed herself in a new outfit, and they went to visit Ma Sybil. Kay was six weeks old. The doorbell rang. "Rena Mae!" Ma Sybil smiled, drying her hands on her apron, and reaching for the small bundle buried in a new pink blanket. Rena Mae blushed foolishly, giggled again and willingly gave Kay up.

"Let me take a good look at my first great-grandchild." Ma Sybil uncovered the baby. Kay squirmed, the petite, corrugated, mass of fiber, was as red as a piece of horsemeat. Kay opened her bird like mouth and yawned. "She's pretty Rena Mae." Ma Sybil expressed, cuddling the tiny child close to her bosom. "What's her name?" "Kay." Rena Mae giggled and followed Ma Sybil into the kitchen.

"She looks exactly like you, when you was this age." Ma Sybil stressed. Rena Mae blushed anew, and in her heart, had hoped that Ma Sybil would keep Kay. The wind was scented with the smell of Magnolia blossoms, the infinite aroma of perfume. Through Ma Sybil's opened kitchen window, clean curtains broke the sunrays, that long strands of threads onto the tablecloth. And the smell of cooking overpowered the subtle perfume of flowers atomizing. Kay cracked opened one eye and sent out a squall.

It was nourishment time for Kay and she dispatched an immediate order. Ma Sybil prepared a bottle for Kay Hannibal, and she cuddled and fed her great-grandchild. "This is a fine baby, Rena Mae." Ma Sybil complimented. "You take good care of her, now." Rena Mae shrank inside of herself. She had wished that Ma Sybil would keep Kay.

"I'll do my best." Rena Mae said finally. "She cries so much. The doctor said she's got gas." "Well babies cry a lot when they are cast into a new environment." Ma Sybil assured. "Just be patient. She'll grow up to be a fine woman." Kay fell asleep immediately in My Sybil's lap, after the feeding.

CHAPTER FOUR

When the rest of the family came home they were glad to see Rena Mae and the baby. They crowded into Ma Sybil's bedroom to get a look at the Kay. Zenna slipped a quarter into the miniature fist. The money stuck out on both sides of the tiny fist. Lulu loved the baby and she too gave the baby a dime. Lulu had wished that Ma Sybil would keep the baby.

Rufus looked at the shriveled mass of flesh and thought to himself that Kay shouldn't have to go through a tough life that he knew she would have to encounter. Rufus also gave Rena Mae two dollars. Rena Mae stayed for dinner, and she was delighted with the juicy meatloaf, hop-in-john, with fresh pods of okra steamed on top. Rena Mae's taste buds zoomed when she sampled her favorite dessert of pungent bread-pudding with whipped cream and nuts on top. Rena Mae left with a clutter of kisses and waves.

5

CHAPTER FIVE

When Rena Mea was almost home, Kay woke-up. She began to screech and squirm. The strong high-pitched sound always made Rena Mae uncomfortable. She didn't know why the sound upset her so, but it did. She was well aware that babies cried and some more than others. But to deal with the constant wailing was something Rena Mae wasn't prepared for. Was it because Kay visualized that the cries focused attention on the mother? One day two older ladies pointed at Rena Mae. "Look! That young girl has a baby." The tallest woman said. "She is just a child herself. Is it her baby?" The other woman asked. No! It's my sister's baby. Rena Mae shot back. "Where is your husband"? Rena Mae recalled in her mind.

At that moment, the diaper bag slipped from Rena Mae's shoulders while, she tried to jiggle the baby quiet. Fruit and some canned milk that Ma Sybil had given her scattered all over the street. Tears flowed down Rena Mae's face, as she tried to retrieve the rolling objects and calm the squawking child at the same time. A husky, tall, young man dressed in overalls, a torn discolored straw hat stained with perspiration, with a grabbing hook hanging from his belt; started collecting the runaway items.

"Hey!" Roger spoke, smiling faintly. "What's this? Do I see a pretty young momma crying?" A smile immediately broke on Rena Mae's face. After all the articles were retrieved and back into the bag, Roger carried the bag. "You live around here?" He inquired.

"Yes!" Rena Mae answered. "I have a room on the next block." "My name is Roger Stark," he said. "I haven't seen you around here, before. Where is your husband?" Rena Mae told

Roger her name and that she didn't have a husband. "How old are you?" Rena Mae answered that too. "My, just a child, you should be home with your mother. Don't you have any folks?" Roger inquired further.

"My mother and father are dead," Rena Mae spoke softly. "My grandmother raised us. I have two sisters and a brother at home with her."

"I see." Roger said, catching hold of Rena Mae's predicament. "I tell you what, I live just around the corner with my folks. Come home with me, my mom knows everything about babies. She can give you some pointers on caring for your baby. You can have dinner with us too. I like you. I would like to see you sometime, that is if you're not already tied up." Roger said all that, without even permitting Rena Mae a chance to answer. "What do you say? Will you come home with me for dinner?" Roger asked, with one foot planted on the bottom step of Rena Mae's house, the diaper still dangling in his hand.

"Yes, I'll go home with you." Rena Mae answered smiling a bit glad that she wouldn't be lonesome and alone with Kay. "But I just had dinner at my grandmother's house. I'm full as a tick."

"Well, my mother is a good cook too." Roger stated smiling back at Rena Mae. "You don't have to eat much. I'm sure that my mother has something cooked that you'll like. Just a taste of whatever you like."

"Ok!" Rena Mae spoke, aware that she would have company for a while.

Roger Stark's father Dan, mother Lizzie, and brother Freddie, all fell in love with Rena Mae and Kay. The Starks were very poor, but very genial people. They were as good as they were poor. The Starks men were all dockworkers. Whenever there was work, one of them worked enough to keep the family going. After dinner, they sat around the table and talked. Rena Mae told them all that happened to her concerning the baby. Mrs. Stark asked to keep the baby while Rena Mae looked for work. They had always wanted a girl, and now, Kay seemed to be the answer to their prayers.

Rena Mae sat prim and prone. She was a subject any artist would give his soul to paint. She was tall, slim, and bore herself stately. Rena Mae's high cheekbones showed that Indian blood was running through her veins. She was self-poised and strode with a dignity that surpassed her sisters. No one was cleaner, neater, or more beautiful. Her starched clean, red and white sundress exposed luscious, brown, plump flesh. Her black hair gleamed from the sunlight. Rena Mae's small arched feet were outfitted with blue and white pumps. A gentle waft of mail order perfume escaped from her body and pervaded the air. She was proud and very selfish. Rena Mae sat there analyzing the station about what to do with Kay.

Jim earned about five dollars a week. After he gave his mother some change, there wasn't much left. Although, Jim pocketed small articles from the drug store; Vaseline, dusting powder, candy, etc... It wasn't enough for two people. Where could Rena Mae find a job, paying enough money for two?

When Rena Mae had reached home, she sat on the bed while Kay had a short nap. She began to ponder the situation anew. Somewhere inside, Rena Mae knew that the Stark's would take good care of Kay. When Kay was three months old, Rena Mae had only twenty-five cents in her possession. She took Kay to a friend's room. The friend didn't work and she roomed with a landlady who worked as a domestic half days and sold liquor and her body the rest of the time.

Rena Mae's friend had her own room and furniture, a second hand bedroom suite, in good condition. The bed was made up with a pretty, clean, pink bedspread. Rena Mae placed Kay in the center of the bed, and then she looked at her friend and laughed. The friend laughed too, but didn't say anything as she sat spellbound, hoping that Kay wouldn't pee on her clean bed spread. Soon the landlady came home with some men who were looking for drinks and love.

The friend, Rena Mae and the baby went to the kitchen with the landlady, where the action was about to take place. Soon Rena Mae left with one of the guys, but she could see that the fellow didn't like the idea of having fun with a baby around. Not too many men would visit her if she had a baby with her.

At first Rena Mae left Kay with the Stark's on a day-to-day basis, hoping that something would happen and she could keep her. Rena Mae took Kay to the Starks every morning, while she was supposed to be looking for work. She was so tried from being up most of the night that, after dropping Kay off, she went back to her room and crawled into bed and went to sleep; sometimes with a companion at her side.

One day, Lizzie and Dan Stark asked Rena Mae for Kay, so that they could give her a home and love. Rena Mae gave in. The Sparks told Rena Mae "we're not asking to adopt Kay, she is your child. Take her whenever you have a home and a job; but let's always be friendly about the situation. Rena Mae you may see Kay anytime you want to. You can take her home with you and spend the night." Rena Mae wondered what it would be like to be to be raised up in a family as bucolic as the Starks. All the Starks could read and write, but the verb busting was something else. Ma Sybil, had always said to them. "You're verb busting, dear! Rephrase that sentence." Ma Sybil would correct them. Rena Mae was practical and she knew that they had to eat and sleep daily and she couldn't afford the service, at that time. So, with all the hard living and the life she liked, without any en-cumbrance; she gave in.

There was a sparse relationship between Rena Mae and Roger. Rena Mae was fond of men who were tall, thin, hand-some, and dressy. Roger wasn't any of the above. Rena Mae was in no position where she was forced to give up some of her self-esteem. But inside, she still did not like gross looking rustic and sloppy dressed men. Rena Mae hated when Roger made love to her. His big, rough scratchy hands felt like sandpaper. Roger's feet sounded like plop-plop when he walked. And the verb busting that caused Rena Mae to recoil. Roger was kind and she wouldn't hurt his feelings.

One thing was for sure, whatever Rena Mae had men sought after it. Rena Mae didn't know or care why everyone didn't have it. She only cared that men swarmed after her like bees. Rena Mae had the power to make others want to be like her. It was the power to her season of life and the time of the year in which she drove that power, as frequency to the airwaves. Rena Mae was never a call girl. That is, she never had a pimp or worked in a madam's house. The men in her life would threaten her bodily harm if they thought she had another man. Rena Mae's style was to shack up with a man and secretly cheat, while accepting gifts from another man. She was always prim and trim. She adored pretty clothes, but she didn't wear hats and never bought one. She was a real clothes addict. She could take or leave alcohol and loved the kind of food that Ma Sybil fed them.

CHAPTER FIVE

"When did you start wearing men's shirts?" Rufus asked, as he stood in her room staring at the expensive shirt.

"That's not for me," Rena Mae smiled. "That is for Tom. Tom lives in the back. One day, I was in the backyard hanging out clothes and he was working in his garden. He fell in love with me right away. We began to talk. And the next day he came to my room and gave me some money. I needed that money. So, when I got some money later, I bought him a shirt. But there's only one thing wrong, he's a married man."

"Married man!" Rufus stated a little shocked. "Rena Mae you better let that woman's husband alone." "He doesn't love her. He loves me." Rena Mae expressed smiling.

"Rena Mae, are you out of your mind?" Rufus exclaimed. "You hardly know Tom. And you say that he doesn't love his wife and he love's you. Is Tom an old man or a young man?" "Middle-aged," Rena Mae stated. "But he's better than some young men in bed."

"That isn't the point Rena Mae." Rufus confirmed. "Tom's probably been married to his wife more than ten years. How can you possibly think that he loves you more than he does his wife? I bet you haven't known Tom two months, yet."

"Well, that's what he tells me." Rena Mae said glumly.

"That is a crafty man." Rufus spoke. "Some men will tell you anything to get what they want. When they get what they want then you don't see them anymore."

"Well, I see him." Rena Mae stated. "He comes to see me almost everyday."

"Rena Mae!" Rufus exclaimed. "Should Tom's wife find out that you're having an affair with her husband, you don't know what she may do to you."

"Tom's wife doesn't know that we see each other." Rena Mae spoke surely. "That's a secret." Rena Mae, stood real and exalted, as if she owned the world.

"Living as close as you do, Tom's wife may somehow find out." Rufus said as he strode from the room.

CHAPTER FIVE

Rufus didn't have to worry about Tom's wife finding out. The landlady approached Rena Mae about so many gentlemen, that she got miffed with the landlady and moved out.

Around twelve o'clock each day Rena Mae arose from her bed regularly. She attended the Star Theater, just across the street from her new home on West Broad Street. She always managed to produce the five-cent fare. Her favorite movie was Mae West's, "Come Up To See Me Sometimes!" Rena Mae often quoted Mae West. She even coined her own phrase. "See you. I got to go turn my "ash-cake!" She would express this when she wanted to break away from a Joe.

Rena Mae enjoyed movies by Johnnie Mack Brown, Bing Crosby, Louise Beaver, Wallace Berry, and Stepin Flecthet. All first run movies were at the Savannah Theater, downtown. The admission fee was fifteen-cents. A place was reserved upstairs for the blacks. Black people called it "Nigger Heaven."

Rena Mae visited the Savannah Theater, once and she declared, never again. Years later the Savannah Theater, was remolded with exquisite red décor and "Nigger Heaven" was no more; integration, don't you know.

Peter Tate, whose acquaintance with Rena Mae had recently made him her first common-law husband. Peter worked at the Union Station, in the baggage department. He had a large airy room with community kitchen privileges. Rena Mae was already behind with her rent, and Peter encouraged her to move in with him. Pete was handsome and Rena Mae liked him. So, early one morning Rena Mae sneaked her belongings out and went to Peter's room. The new address and the new way of life kept Rena Mae busy and away from Jim, the baby's father and Roger Stark; where the baby now lived.

Jim soon left Savannah. He went to live with relatives in Newark, New Jersey. He wanted a better paying job. After he had a job, he wrote Rena Mae and he put a few bills in the envelop for the baby. When Rena Mae finally got around to answering Jim's letter, it was returned, marked unknown. Years later, a relative of Jim's told Rena Mae that Jim had married and had a son.

Spring had arrived. The cool air tingled the nose. The trees were budding with green leaves. The birds flew lively about, while the wind blew warmly; a sign that springtime was really in. Peter Tate, loved pretty women, and many prostitutes hung out at the railroad station, where he worked. Peter had an affair with one of them and he became infected with syphilis. In a short time the disease was transmitted to Rena Mae, and two cysts showed up in her abdominal region. The cysts were very painful. Rena Mae decided to prick them with a needle so the puss would drain out. She purchased a pack of needles, sterilized them over a flame, and opened both lumps. But no puss came out, just fluid. The fluid continued to seep out, and caused her clothing to be wet at times. The pain didn't decrease either. In fact, it became steadily worse. All the medication that she had brought, plus the medicine that Peter had brought from the job dispensary failed to heal the open sores. Rena Mae began to lose weight, she was very sick and she dropped out of sight. A friend suggested that she visit a clinic.

The day was dry. The broiling sun hung in the clear sky, its ominous rays could be seen everywhere on the parched earth. Early that morning Rena Mae arrived at the clinic before it was opened. Already, two lines lapped around the block, one for whites and the other for blacks. Syphilis was on the rampage in Savannah that year. Of course, not all people in the line were syphilis cases. The temperature soared, and the early morning sun hit Rena Mae directly on her hatless head, beating down on her like a club. Rena Mae began to perspire profusely. She swayed and staggered while in line. A person guided her to the front line where a shed extended over some rough, huge, wooden benches.

Rena Mae was in such a distressed, weakened condition, that a man arose from his seat and offered his place to her. Half an hour later, the clinic was officially opened and two at a time from the double line flowed in. Two young, white scary looking nurses stood on the far side of the room and pointed to the table where the patients were to lie on.

When the doctor asked the nurses for an object, the doctor had to give a long arm reach. The nurses displayed a behavior, as though the disease would leap from the patient and attack them. As one of the suffering was undressing to be examined, the patient simply flashed the spot that was affected with open sores. After a quick look, the doctor gave out pills, and rub on medication, and dismissed the patient. "Come back in two weeks." The doctor ordered.

The treatment from the clinic didn't help Rena Mae. One day as she hobbled from a food store, she met a friend who wanted to know what was wrong with her. Rena Mae had changed so much, by that point, that all modesty had flown from her. All she wanted was, to be well again. Rena Mae told her friend everything about her sickness, the medication from the clinic and the pricking of the cysts.

"You're wasting your time, dear." The friend spoke. "I had a similar condition. I know a crack-shot West Indian doctor who cured me. This doctor will examine you without any charge. He'll tell you what the problem is and how much it will cost."

The friend insisted that Rena Mae visit the very important doctor. The next day Rena Mae limped to see this extraordinary physician. "These two lumps are hernias." The doctor explained. "Somebody had his dirty dick inside you. Did you open the cysts?" Rena Mae said that she had. "Now, the damn germs have penetrated them." The doctor spoke.

"Do you know who gave you this disease?" The physician questioned.

"Yes, my husband." Rena Mae answered. She wouldn't tell the doctor that he was her common-law husband.

"Well! He'd better get his sore ass to the doctor, fast!" The medic stated. "Or you'll never get well." "The doctor on his job is treating him." Rena Mae said barely audible.

CHAPTER FIVE

"Very well!" added the medic, staring at Rena Mae inquiringly. "As long as he is being treated. These hernias must be burned out, before they'll heal." "Burned out!" Rena Mae exclaimed, alarm written all over her face.

"Yes, my dear." The doctor voiced. "And with a red hot iron. Of course, you won't feel it. I'll anesthetize the area. It'll take about an hour or so. You'll rest a while after the operation. Then you may go home. The operation will cost ten dollars in advance."

Rena Mae thanked the doctor and got dressed. "I'll be back tomorrow." She assured the doctor. Rena Mae didn't have a cent in the world. But she knew that she must have ten dollars by tomorrow. Rena Mae just couldn't stand the pain any longer and she had to get well. Rena Mae's mind floated to her family. Uncle Albert and Aunt Callie were always so kind t her, but she couldn't let any of her family know. She had some pride left. And too, maybe, they would say I told you so. No, there must be another way, she thought.

Though Rena Mae was weak, and in pain; she still managed to prepare dinner for Peter. When Peter came home, she related the whole episode about what the doctor had said. Peter was penniless also and sick, but he continued to work everyday. Peter had a friend who lived twenty miles away. He knew that his friend would loan him ten dollars. So after dinner he started the journey on foot. Sometime after midnight Peter had made the forty-mile track.

A storm was brewing. Black clouds grew and ascended in the sky, their dark outlines changed as Rena Mae watched through the windowpane. Peter had left and Rena Mae was lying in bed her body contorted in pain. A restless breeze shivered through the dark trees. In the apex the thunder muttered viciously and angrily, all by itself. The sharp lightening snapped and popped viciously. Rena Mae for the first time since she left home was afraid. She regretted her passive resistance toward her family and wished that she had heeded Ma Sybil's warnings. Rena Mae didn't seem to be a part of anything. She was like a puffball; if you nudged it with your toes, it would fly away to nothing. She had managed to push anyone back when she was crowed, except Ma Sybil. Ma Sybil dreaded the thought Rena Mae would go the way her mother had gone.

Although, Rena Mae was anesthetized, she could faintly feel a muffled sensation. Although, the smell of burning flesh, sickened her even more, she tried to be brave; in fact she was brave. She didn't flinch but her mouth quivered. Rena Mae rolled her eyes from which streams of tears flowed downward, warming her cheeks. She could hear the tears splash onto the white paper that covered the table. When it was all over the doctor bound up her wounds and led her to a small room to rest. Rena Mae's leg belonged to someone else, she thought. She felt as though she was a hundred years old.

Rena Mae must have dozed off. She opened her eyes to the doctor's nudging her on her arm. "You may get dressed now!" The tall handsome middle-aged, copper tone doctor assisted Rena Mae by lifting her under the arms. The doctor helped

her to dress and he gave her a light tap on the rump. "Chin-up."
He said. "Don't worry, you'll soon be well and having a good
time again." The doctor encouraged. The operation irritated Rena Mae so much that even her hearing was impaired. She
groaned lightly looking fearfully at the doctor. Her gaze was like
a hare snared in a trap.

Hot, clear weather had followed thunder, lightening and
downpours that drenched the city. Suddenly, a slight breeze was
blowing and radiant sunshine filtered through quivering leaves.
Rena Mae didn't even have ten cents to hire a Yellow Cab that
would have deposited her at her door. As she moved, her long
spidery legs block after block, she sometimes walked sideways.
Rena Mae was an old invalid edging up the staircase. She
stopped to rest now and then. The wound was so very painful, it
seemed as if everything in the world was pressing against it.
There was grave pressure, magnifying the incision, causing despair and hysteria.

CHAPTER FIVE

Rena Mae was a charming, beautiful young girl who was too anxious for a life of pleasure. She was too young to know the ways of the world and how to avoid its pitfalls. And yet, so artful that some people couldn't find it in their hearts to condemn her. But felt only pity and sympathy, for her. As Rena Mae struggled down the street, from the doctor's office, she was a truly pathetic figure. She was shabbily dressed, hardly more than a ghost of her former self.

A man sweeping the sidewalk in front of his house watched Rena Mae as she posed herself against a tree to rest. "Are you sick lady?" The man questioned. "Can I help? You can come in and sit on the porch." ventured the man as he glared at Rena Mae's worn and perturbed looking body.

"No, I'll be all right." Rena Mae answered, thanking him and waving him away. "I just need to rest a while." She spoke, her eyes piercing the sidewalk and fleeting the man's head. "I can walk with you, if you like!" The Good Samaritan said. "You can lean on me for support." "No, that isn't necessary," Rena

Mae frowned. "Thanks anyway." The man said something else, but Rena Mae didn't hear him. She didn't listen, and she didn't answer. Get away from me, you shit-ass, damn fool, she thought. That's all I need. For you to talk me to death and proposition me for some pussy, she reflected.

In the arena of Rene Mae's mind she felt as though she wouldn't ever feel anything again. Sensitive, hard-boiled, Rena Mae was almost breathless, as she limped on and did not look back. Sick as she was she again prepared Peter's dinner, navy beans cooked with neck-bones, cracked rice, and Kool-Aid.

Rena Mae in her extreme wildness had alienated herself from her family. After sometime, with no communication with Rena Mae, Ma Sybil appealed to Rufus to look her up. He knew Rena Mae frequented a ten-cent dancehall on West Broad Street. Rena Mae loved to dance and she was good at it.

Toward evening, a heavy summer thunderstorm gathered. The massive racing, low clouds seemed as though they would touch the tall buildings. Furious winds lashed at every-

132

thing, and the rain poured. From upstairs, Rufus could hear the sound of revelry, in the street. Rena Mae wasn't dancing that night; she wasn't even there and hadn't been for some time. A comrade of Rena Mae's directed Rufus to her quarters. When Rufus had rooted Rena Mae out, he was shocked. His young, sassy, beautiful sisters, cadaver-like features loomed before him. Rena Mae blushed crimson, like a child found out. Her eyelids weighted down as if pressed by a steelyard. When she smiled, a dime could've easily been completely, hidden in her deep dimples. Rena Mae and Rufus greeted each other. They sat down and Rufus took a pack of cigarettes from his pocket. He put a cigarette into his mouth, lit it, and tossed the pack to Rene Mae; she accepted. Rufus sat leaning with his elbow on the chair's arm and holding the smoke in his right hand. He gazed at his sister and tears welled up in his eyes. Rufus looked away because he could see that Rena Mae was under very strained circumstances. Rena Mae's eyes fell on Rufus like a giant prune hanging from a limb.

Rena Mae was doing all that she could to rehabilitate her weak, frail body; but she was still a sick woman. She was tough and she tried to be strong. She sat smoking, wanting to scratch the itch from her operation, spreading a fiery, tormenting feeling beneath her skirt. On Rena Mae's forehead were little beads of sweat. She wiped them off with the back of her hand. She talked poignantly about the events in her life and the operation. Tears were slowly crawling down her withered cheeks. Rena Mae gave Rufus a side-glance. And for a while, they were silent, as though paying respect to the memory of the dead. At that moment Rena Mae wished that Rufus would take her home. But the idea was suppressed because she didn't want give the rest of the family, what she had. The doctor said that the disease was contagious.

Rufus spoke softly as was his way. He stood up and looked down at Rena Mae like a worried mother cow, gazing at its offspring who was down and couldn't rise to its feet. "Rena Mae, get a room all by yourself!" The words were impressive.

Rena Mae took another cigarette to torture her body. "You're not in any condition to be living with a man." Rufus strode to Rena Mae and gave her some money. "This'll tide you until next week. Find a room immediately," he pleaded. Rufus bent down and kissed Rena Mae on the top of her head. "Drop us a card of your new address. We'll help you until you're well again. I'm not trying to run your life, but you better slow down a bit. Why do you move so often?" Rufus wanted to know.

"Well, sometimes the landlady complains about things." Rena Mae said. "When she does, I just move out. And too, I need to ditch a man that I'm tired of." Rena Mae reported. "I see. But I still say take it easy." Rufus spoke. Rena Mae who was always haughty, carefree, gay, a real foul mouth, with so much pluck, now subdued and pathetic. Tears hung on Rufus' eyelids somehow he restrained them. Time sure had set its hand upon Rena Mae, he thought. "I guess that would be best." She finally spoke, waving her right hand methodically in the air. "Especially, since my family's going to help me."

After Rufus left, Rena Mae looked into the mirror. It gave her back her face, and she didn't like what she saw. Rena Mae got dressed and went to locate a room. She had no trouble finding a nice, clean, airy one. The location was not far from where Kay, her baby, lived with the Starks.

Rena Mae returned to the room she shared with Peter. She cleaned the room, cooked, washed and ironed Peter's clothes. She then packed her belongings, hailed a taxi, and directed him to her new abode. Rena Mae didn't even leave Peter a note.

CHAPTER SIX

Rufus detailed Rena Mae's condition to the rest of the family. They were teary-eyed and sad. The family gave Rufus money for Rena Mae, Lulu, the youngest child, even emptied her piggybank and sent the money to her sister.

The week after Rena Mae's operation, she returned to the doctor for treatment. She sat in the waiting room until she was called. "How do you feel today?" The doctor asked. "Better! I don't have much pain now, but the itching is annoying." Rena Mae said.

"That means the sores are healing." The doctor returned. "Where is the money?" He asked. "I don't have any money today," Rena Mae explained sadly. "I'll bring it next week."

"Well, you come back when you have the money." The doctor said harshly. "You don't think that I'm going to work on these dirty sores for nothing, do you?"

Rena Mae sat transfixed. It was as though a dark cloud had covered her. She couldn't understand how the doctor, who was so kind and had helped her so much, just a week ago, could be mean and rude today. After her stunned feelings had passed, and she noticed the miracle doctor standing glaring down at her, Rena Mae said. "Yes sir." She slowly pulled herself up from the chair and left.

When Rena Mae finally reached the street, she thought, what happened to the doctor's Hippocratic oath? Did he think that she wouldn't pay the two dollars? He wasn't hard up. He had a big business, a car, and his own home, she thought. What's wrong with people? She continued to reminisce. Rena Mae was in a dazed condition until the hot sun bearing down on her head pulled her back to reality. Is this what life is really about? She wondered. Now I can understand why my mother committed suicide. This world isn't easy to live in, especially for poor people. For a split second Rena Mae thought further, my mother had her mother, Ma Sybil, and the rest of the family to take us. Should I kill myself, Kay would be cut off from the family forever. I want Kay to know me and be a part of my family. I'll never go back to that doctor. I'll die first, she thought.

Rena Mae stumbled with her thoughts. She passed a drugstore, went inside and bought a bottle of iodine and a bottle of Mercurochrome. Ma Sybil had always used that medication on the children for cuts and bruises. Rena Mae went home and dressed her wounds and went to sleep. She had little pain after the operation, but the itching was uncomfortable. Rena Mae wanted to scratch all the time, but couldn't. So she pressed the spot as hard as she could and suffered the rest.

The edges of the tress blazed with purple light and their middle gradually turned from deep violet to ebony. From Rena Mae's window a light breeze stirred but she stayed in bed, trying to stabilize her sick body. Rufus visited his sister often and some of Rena Mae's cronies passed by weekly and gave her a dollar. When Rena Mae felt and looked better she went to the Starks to see her child, Kay. One day Rena Mae visited the Starks, and when she left she took Kay with her to spend the night.

Kay was now, crawling and into everything. Rena Mae had thrown some the used bandages into the fireplace to be burned. Kay crawled into the fireplace and discovered the bandages and rubbed them against her stomach, around the navel area. Rena Mae took Kay back the next day, but during the day Kay became ill and blisters broke out on her stomach. The Starks took Kay to the doctor, who questioned them as to where the child had been. Of course, they told him about Rena Mae's trouble. The doctor treated the baby and stipulated that under no circumstances was Kay to visit her mother again, until she was well. The Starks relayed the message to Rena Mae. She agreed to come and see Kay but would not take her to her living quarters.

CHAPTER SIX

Rena Mae's operation took sometime to heal. The deep cavities had to fill up with flesh, and healed over. But in time, with youth and perseverance, she did shake off the illness. Once again, Rena Mae was fresh, vibrant and as new as tomorrow. She wasn't completely the same though. The sickness left her with a slight limp and a poise that made her seem to lean forward when she stood. Rena Mae was still an attractive woman, but now she was considered a six o' clock woman instead of a woman with big hips, as she had called them "my big hips."

The stars disappeared in a bright haze. The moon, not yet full shone with a steady brilliance. Its light washed over the sky in a pale blue flood and it threw a misty golden stain on the thin clouds sailing near it. Around midnight, Rufus was making it home with his footsteps ringing the empty stillness, and echoed clearly from the pavement. Suddenly, Rufus' ears picked up a melodious lament. West Broad Street seemed to rise under his feet. Then he heard feet rapidly beating the ground.

Rufus stopped and waited to see what it was all about. The cries had ceased with an unexpected abruptness, and Rena Mae's countenance was grave as she stood face to face with her brother. "I've been robbed!" Rena Mae yelled, breathing hard and dabbing at her eyes. "You've been robbed?" Rufus inquired, gazing at his sister's disheveled attire. "What you doing in this alley, anyway? How much money did you loose?" "Twenty dollars!" Rena Mea frowned embarrassed, smoothing down her hair. "What in the world were you doing with that kind of money on you?" Rufus asked, looking at Rena Mae as she stood before him. "Well, you see, it was like this." Rena Mae began to explain. "I met two handsome, middle-aged, well dressed, black men, and they asked me for a date. Both of them wanted to date me. They gave me the twenty-dollar bill. Ten dollars a piece, that's a lot of money." Rena Mae spoke, as the veins stood out on her temple, pulsating rapidly. "I had the wampum, right there in my hand." She held out her hand and pointed where the money had lain. "Then one guy said, now you're a nice, pretty young

young girl, and we don't want anything to happen to your money. This is a very exciting business, you know. Should a cop happen to come by or we split up, you meet us in Jason's Bar around the corner." Rena Mae's eyes expanded as she spoke.

"Rena Mae! You don't let anyone hold your money." Rufus spoke. "Well, I trusted them." Rena Mae said tearfully. "Now, I don't have anything. All my money is gone. They ran with my money." Man number one, arose from Rena Mae's body, fastened his trousers and took charge of the money; not even looking at his comrade. He stepped aside with a sheepish grin, to make room for his colleague. When the second man had finished his act, he arose to his feet shouting, Police! Police! Here comes the police and took off running. "Did you go into the bar?" Rufus inquired, angrily. "No, I was too frightened. I jumped up so fast I almost tripped over my bloomers. I looked about but I didn't see any police. I was afraid to go into the bar. The police may be there and arrest me."

The coolness of the air made her eyes slightly moist. Rufus raised his hands, his fingers stirred as though he was playing on an invisible instrument. He started on a string of reproaches. "Rena Mae! You've been had; flim-flamed!" That's what they called it in the hip world. "Why don't you get a job and stop this dirty business?" Rena Mae and Yamacraw were constantly hyphened between Rufus. He was as cross as an interstate junction. At that moment Rufus hated Rena Mae. He hated the hurt that she represented; in spite of the sickness, Rena Mae hadn't learned anything.

"Rena Mae! Get a job!" Rufus shouted, a little out of control.

"You talk like a damn fool!" Rena Mae snapped back, her disposition far out of proportion to the effect involved. "Don't give me your superior attitude. You're a pimp, and don't try to deny it. Where do you get all those new clothes and shiny shoes? Ma Sybil, certainly don't buy them for you. You don't make that much money cutting hair."

CHAPTER SIX

"No, Ma Sybil don't buy them and neither do anyone else." Rufus stated feeling his patience straining. "I work at various jobs, you know. As for me being a pimp, that's a lie. Pimps take women's money and beat them. The only woman I struck, in my entire life was you. When you took my fountain pen, and gave it away. I am a bouncer, at a house where parties are held and I get paid for my service." Rufus spoke harshly. "Rena Mae! Get a job!" He shouted again.

"There aren't any damn jobs to be had!" Rena Mae shouted back. "Oh there are jobs." Rufus informed. "You can get a job at the CCC cleaning vacant lots for the city." "You expect me to work for the CCC!" Rena Mae shouted. "To work as a field nigger, cutting down trees all day! Blistering my hands and scratching my legs! One day Aunt Callie took me to the hotel to do a day's work for a cracker woman, she asked me to pass her something and my hand mistakenly touched hers. She drew back her hand as if a bee had stung her. She rubbed her hand on her apron to erase the poison I had transplanted; which made the insult so much worst. Get a job my ass! I'll sell my pussy from now on." Rena Mae scowled as she stomped her foot on the pavement.

"Well, from what you've just told me." Rufus rolled his eyes and jammed his hands deep into his pockets. "You sure make a poor salesperson." Rena Mae's mind is like an automatic trap, once closed, no amount of persuading would open it, he thought.

"Well, I guess you want me to work for that woman at the hotel." Rena Mae flew at Rufus. "That bitch gave me seventy-five cents for a whole days work, and some of her husband's old shoes and shirts. What in the hell could I do with that shit! I didn't know anyone they would fit. Those things would only fit a midget anyway. So I put them in the first trashcan, I saw. I can at least make a few dollars in a short time."

"Lizzie Starks works for the CCC." Rufus commented, hoping that Rena Mae would realize her shameful state. "It's good enough for Lizzie, and the money certainly would support your child. No doubt, sometimes, you do go there and eat too."

"What?" Rena Mae was wound up like a mechanical doll gone out of control. "That work suits Lizzie Starks. She's an old ugly woman. I'm young and pretty. I will never work on that job. I'm a woman not a man." "Well then, why not let Zenna teach you to type?" Rufus said, still trying to convince Rena Mae to find a job. "Zenna earns money typing letters for people. You could too."

"Zenna doesn't have to teach me anything." Rena Mae snapped sarcastically, adjusting her belt around her small waist. "I already have it in me." "That stands to be seen." Rufus said hostilely. "Anyway, you should let it work itself out. I hope to-night's episode will be a lesson for you. Now you know that you can be conned more than one way." Rufus cooled it when things became overheated. He gave Rena Mae some coins and advised her to go home. He knew that was like asking Rena Mae to climb a glass wall. Rena Mae's teeth chattered, and she went stumbling along. They departed and both ambled in their separate ways.

7

CHAPTER SEVEN

Zenna was the second child, intelligent, good-natured, pretty and very helpful to Ma Sybil in every way. Zenna seemed to know the great burden her grandmother was enduring. Ma Sybil had the whole responsibility of the house and the children. Zenna was always busy around the house. She did whatever to alleviate the tasks from her grandmother.

When Zenna was sitting her hands were busy knitting, crocheting, or embroidering. Ma Sybil and the rest of the family would rest on the front porch, talking to neighbors who passed. Ma Sybil glanced around, "Zenna! Where are you?" Ma Sybil inquired. "I'm cleaning the pantry shelves, Ma Sybil." Zenna spoke. "Zenna! Come sit down, with us." Ma Sybil instructed. "You're not a slave, you know. You don't need to work every waking moment. The pantry can wait. Come sit with us."

Zenna strode over to Ma Sybil and planted a kiss on her brow. "Bless you Ma Sybil," she said. "I was trying to take some of the load off you." Zenna explained as she sat down with some sewing material to work on. Zenna was the only one of the children who finished high school. Ma Sybil was proud of her. She bought Zenna a second hand sewing machine. And when she graduated, Ma Sybil bought Zenna a new typewriter.

Zenna loved the machine and was very thankful for it. She took typing lessons and learned to care for the machine. She typed letters for the neighbors and she wrote poems and short stories. Zenna's favorite writers were Pushkin, Lord Byron, Phyllis Wheatly, and Ezra Pond.

Her instructor said that her poems were good and she should publish them, but Zenna never submitted any of her work for publication.

"The Pigeon"

The pigeon is dead,

It had spread its wings,

The marks were there in the snow.

The eyes stared fixedly,

As if one last look

At the cruel world in New York City.

"To Joyce"

Tall and erect

Face of a fawn

Lovely palms

You are brisk, crisp, and concise

You are in demand

A kind of a healing hand

You are a friend.

THE CROSSING OF YAMACRAW

Life in Yamacraw, continued in its invigorated order. On weekdays the dark abominable labor consumed the common people's time; and on Sunday mornings Yamacraw families poured in droves into the churches. Timmy Pettigrew worshipped at the same church as Zenna and her family. Since Timmy Pettigrew came to Savannah, from Waycross, Georgia, he was a dutiful member. At first he was an usher, and soon became captain of the usher board. Timmy was a good worker in the church. Ma Sybil was brought up in that same church. She had seen many members come and go, some to glory, and others just left.

Timmy first saw Zenna at church; she sang a solo one Sunday. Her voice and her beauty entrapped Timmy and he fell in love with her. One Sunday after services, Timmy asked Zenna if it was all right to walk her home, and she said it was ok. That was the beginning of Timmy Pettigrew and Zenna Hannibal's love affair. Ma Sybil liked Timmy, because he was so polite and helpful. One day Ma Sybil was struggling with a board that had fallen off her fence. Timmy, who was passing by, took the hammer from Ma Sybil's hands and nailed the board to its foundation. After that, Ma Sybil's respect for Timmy's manners increased.

When Timmy asked for Zenna's hand in marriage, Ma Sybil thought it was a very good idea. Of course they had to discuss the matter. Besides, Ma Sybil had a sorrowful phobia about Rena Mae. At least Zenna would be protected, she thought.

"Timmy's illiterate!" Rufus spoke. "He's thirty-five years old and Zenna is just nineteen." Although Zenna loved her brother, at that moment she cursed him in her heart. She thought he was throwing a wedge in her wedding path. "Because Timmy is illiterate, Ma Sybil spoke as she sat primly on the edge of her chair, "doesn't mean that he isn't a good person, Rufus. Timmy is polite and he has been on the same job since he came to Savannah. Timmy does not read or write, but he can count money and numbers in his head as well as any mathematician. I heard that Timmy's boss asked him to cut a piece of lumber, and he cut the exact size he was told to." Ma Sybil said softly as she rested her back against her chair.

"Well, that may be good." Rufus stated. "But it doesn't tell us what kind of person he is, his character." "He certainly is a good worker in the church," Ma Sybil continued. "Timmy started as an usher and now he's captain of the usher board. Whenever there's a drive to raise money for the church, Timmy leads. Most of his co-workers donate generously, even his boss gives."

"True, Timmy's thirty-five and Zenna is much younger," Uncle Albert interpreted. "Rufus, you must look at the advantage point." Uncle Albert puffed on his cigarette and eyed Rufus directly. "Zenna says she loves Timmy and he loves her and that is good. Timmy has a job and a two room flat." Uncle Albert waited for Rufus to reply, but Rufus didn't reply just then. Aunt Callie spoke up.

"Rufus, you want Zenna to be happy, don't you?" Aunt Callie returned. "Zenna will have a roof over her head and food and clothes as well. Now-a-days, that's something to shout about."

"Yes. Yes, I want Zenna to be happy." Rufus finally expressed, his eyes tracing a dirt dauber that had just flown in, as Lulu opened the door. The insect had a small ball of mud in its mouth, searching for the perfect landscape for its home. "There is something about the guy that I don't like. It seems as if he's holding something back," Rufus explained. Ma Sybil offered an encouraging smile at Zenna, along with a nod of the head, while words flew back and forth.

Lulu posed by the door, waiting for a break in the conversation so that she could ask permission to take a fruit. The break came. "Excuse me! Ma Sybil, may I have a fruit?" Lulu said. "Yes, just one not the whole bunch," Ma Sybil made clear. "Yes mam." Lulu dashed for the kitchen where the fruit was kept. She took a pear, bit into it, and ambled back into the living room crunching the edible. Lulu glanced around the group. She had heard enough to know whom the conversation was about.

155

"Why so much fuss over a man, who was made in the bushes?" Lulu exclaimed.

"Lulu!" Ma Sybil announced harshly, which caused tears to cascade down Lulu's cheeks. Zenna's ears popped as she stared into space. For a moment Zenna heard a loud, unpleasant buzzing sound, which made her feel dizzy and slightly sick.

"I'm sorry Ma Sybil." Lulu spoke lamely. "The children said that Timmy was made in the bushes." Zenna shocked, rushed over to Lulu and put her arms around her sister to comfort her. "It's alright Lulu," Zenna said. "You are only repeating what you heard."

"You should be sorry." Ma Sybil chastised Lulu, frowning a bit. "If I wasn't busy here, I would wash your mouth out with soap and water. Go outside and play; don't repeat what you hear." Lulu sadly dragged herself out of the room nibbling on the pear.

"My! The child knows more than I thought she did." Ma Sybil stated. "They all do." Aunt Callie followed up. "Children do grow up, you know, and very fast."

"Yes, now let us get back to the subject." Ma Sybil spoke. "Rufus, I didn't say that I was convinced that Timmy is the right man for Zenna, nor that Zenna couldn't have done better. I do think that we should give it a chance, especially since they love each other."

"Okay," Rufus answered timidly. "Since Timmy is so much older than Zenna, he might be a good husband, after all." But Rufus still had his doubts.

After the approval of Zenna's wedding had been established, Zenna's small feet carried her across the room. She kissed each person in the room and then exclaimed, "I am happy! I am happy!" "We are happy for you," everyone said in unison.

"Zenna, you are a good person and you deserve the best." Ma Sybil stated. Her eyes were misty, as she thought; at least

Zenna turned out to be a lady. "Take care of your husband and home, Zenna." Ma Sybil concluded.

"I will! I will!" Zenna joyfully beamed, as she invisibly hugged herself, thinking how wonderful it would be to be Timmy's wife. Ma Sybil had no intention to race with nature. She knew when her hormones came to stimulate. Every person couldn't handle it. Ma Sybil had not forgotten Rena Mae's plight.

CHAPTER EIGHT

On a beautiful, hot Sunday in June, Ma Sybil, the family, and friends made the last minute preparations for Zenna's wedding. The wedding was held at the church after the regular service was over. Rufus gave the bride away. Zenna, young and beautiful, felt like an astronaut before taking off for the moon. Her heart throbbed wildly and she could not keep her mind fixed on anything. Zenna's heart was anxious; its door was standing wide open. Timmy Pettigrew was tall, dark and graceful. He was also ready, his adams apple stood out like a cock's plumage, and at times it bounced up and down.

After the wedding ceremony, guests jammed Ma Sybil's home, where tables were piled high with spicy, succulent food. Plenty of wine and Homebrew were at the guest's disposal. The bed was also heaped with presents. Timmy's boss sent a beautiful spread. Rena Mae managed to bring a nice gift, a set of monogrammed pillowcases.

Timmy was especially debonair to all. As Zenna cut the cake, Timmy placed his oversized peasant hands on top of Zenna's bird like hands. Then he filled the glasses with wine and passed them around. Timmy toasted his bride and the guests. After the feast, the bride and groom and some young visitors strode to the decorated, big backyard. They gaily skipped and hopped to the tune of a guitar.

When the party was over, Zenna left her family and went home with her husband. Someday, they would have a family of their own, Zenna thought. Before they were married Timmy had said that he wanted Zenna to teach him to read and write. Zenna thought that it was a splendid idea and she was willing to help her husband in anyway she could. To instruct Timmy to be astute would be as joyful as teaching her own children, when they arrived, she thought.

Timmy was a laborer, who had no skills or academic training. He was extremely jealous of Zenna's education. He tried to hold her back, like barnacles under a ship. Zenna had tremendous courage and pride that staggered Timmy's imagination. The thing that Timmy was trying to break was gigantic and as solid as the rock of Gibraltar. After the marriage, Timmy changed his mind about Zenna teaching him to read and write. Zenna did not think much about it. She thought that Timmy would later change his mind. She continued to be a good wife and homemaker. She also helped Ma Sybil with the lunches as it was agreed, before the marriage. It was Zenna's idea. She wanted to help Ma Sybil who had made life so comfortable and worthwhile for them.

Zenna and Timmy had three months of total bliss. Zenna loved Timmy with all her heart, and she thought he was handsome. She didn't think less of Timmy because of his background. Zenna loved Timmy for himself. Three months after the marriage, Timmy forbade Zenna to leave the house without him. Timmy's inferiority complex was most damaging for himself. Through the clean opened windowpane, miniature dust particles danced in horizontal beams that streamed through the clean opened window. It was a fine day in Savannah, yet Zenna didn't notice it as she sat gazing yet not seeing the magnificent phenomenon. Surely, Timmy's mood would change, she thought. Zenna tried to convince Timmy that her family loved him and accepted him and wanted him around. "My family loves you, Timmy. Do you think my family would have agreed for me to marry you if they disliked you?"

"They don't like me!" Timmy shouted, while washing up for dinner. Behind Timmy's hostile badinage, there was a sneer in his eyes. Timmy made a gesture of impatience. "My Uncle Louis and Aunt Sarah, who raised me, are the only people who really love me. My birth mother didn't love me. She left me when I was only two months old. She never wrote a single line, and she could write. She didn't even send me a pair of drawers to cover my black ass. How could a woman give birth to a child and walk away from the child and never look back? That's beyond me! I would like to see her and tell her that and some other things too."

Timmy was reminiscing. His face was ashen and the veins stood out on each side of his neck, as he sat down at the table to eat. "Well, I can understand about your mother." Zenna put in. "My mother left us also when she committed suicide. If it were not for our grandmother, we would have been in the same situation."

"No you don't understand!" Timmy shouted, distorting his face. "No one understands and could never understand. Your grandmother lives in the city and she can read and write. You went to school in the city; I had to walk five miles to go to school. When I went there, the children laughed at me. My oversized shoes, jacket, shirt, all was too big. I was a sight. Your mother is dead. My mother is alive. A friend of the family saw her and talked to her last year. She was living in Key West, Florida, with a man. She said that he was her husband."

Zenna, not knowing what ground to tread on, ventured slowly and softly. "Timmy, I love you." Zenna waited for an answer. "I am sure that my family loves you too. Anyway, you are married to me, not my family." Zenna concluded.

"If you love me," Timmy cocked his head to one side, "then you will do as I say. Visit no one. We don't need anyone. We have each other."

"Timmy, we must attend church." Zenna tried again. "Yes." Timmy agreed to that. "But we don't need to visit peoples houses."

"What peoples houses are you talking about?" Zenna questioned. "We only visit my grandmother's home." Timmy was so empty that he could fall a hundred miles within himself and he would never reach bottom, Zenna thought. "I love my family and I had hoped that you would accept my family as yours."

"You see that proves it," Timmy shouted, his brow furrowed. "You really don't give a damn about me. All you want is a roof over your head."

Zenna searched her mind's eye for reason. "My grandmother sacrificed a great deal for me, for all of us. And not to visit her, would be ungrateful and wicked." "Another thing, that son-of-a-bitch, brother of yours, he hates my guts!" Timmy yelled. "He thinks that I am not good enough for his sister. You finished high school and I can't read and write. He may not say he hates me, but I know he does. A man knows another man."

"Timmy, I think you're highly exaggerating the whole episode." Zenna spoke softly, trying to appease Timmy's feelings.

"Don't throw them high blown words at me." Timmy bellowed, his breathing rising sharply. "You're trying to make small of me. I know that I can't read and write." Timmy was like a child who picked up a bedroom utensil and not knowing its purpose.

"I will teach you to read and write." Zenna said piously. "You said before we were married, that you wanted me to teach you to read and write."

"You can't teach me anything!" Timmy thundered, vociferously. "You're so high and mighty. You think you know everything. I count figures in my head, faster than you can with a pencil and I can count money too. A typewriter! Who are you going to write that is so important that you can't write with a pencil?"

Zenna nervously sat at the table, while Timmy muttered on. His big nostrils were flaring in moments of strong emotions. Zenna aged by the minute, and then by the hour. She was vain and decided to deal with the insults by ignoring Timmy. She wanted to break that storm rumbling and thumping within him. Timmy was in a state of complete panic. He's a devil even before he goes to hell, she thought. Were all husbands like this?

Were her father and grandfather like this? Zenna did not remember much about them. She glanced at Timmy as he sat at the table before her. Fright crowded closely on Zenna's heels. Timmy's sharp eyes, his thick lipped mouth, tough black hair, six-three frame, his set piercing eyes, that looked as though they would bore a hole right through her. His trumpet voice loomed up at her and frightened her. Zenna screwed up her face into a scowl, like she smelled some foul odor and began to eat her dinner as Timmy continued to badger her.

After two days of isolation, Zenna went to see her family. She related the whole episode to Ma Sybil. "Well, dear, Timmy is jealous of your family ties." Ma Sybil pacified Zenna. "He doesn't have a family, you do, and he resents it. Timmy had a rough life. Be tolerant with him. He will come around. Take this sweet potatoes pie to him. He loves them. Tell him that Ma Sybil made it especially for him. This should assure him that your family loves him."

That same evening Timmy and Zenna sat to eat dinner. "Timmy, Ma Sybil sent you this pie," Zenna smiled, pushing the pastry towards Timmy. "Granny made it especially for you. She told me to tell you so." Timmy stared at the pie and Zenna. His jaws were set like granite, his eyes cold and hard. Zenna looked at him, shrank inside and waited.

"I thought I told you not to leave this house!" Timmy roared. "Timmy!" Zenna began, but he did not wait for her to speak further. He knocked the sweet potato pie and all the food to the floor with one scoop. He stood up, his eyes aflame and frost began to form at the corners of his mouth. Timmy pivoted on his heels and knocked the typewriter to the floor.

"What you need a typewriter for?" Timmy paused. "Who you got to write too, so important that you must type the letters and the fucking poems?" Timmy ran to the dresser drawers where Zenna had so neatly and tenderly placed them. Timmy tore them up. What good do them poems do you?" Timmy's hands swiftly went across Zenna's face. He grabbed her shoulders, touching her in a rough, ugly way. He was physically abusing and degrading Zenna.

"Timmy!" Zenna screamed at last. Are you losing your mind?" What has come over you? You must know that I won't live like this. You must be crazy!"

"Crazy huh?" Timmy began fidgeting and fumbling for words. "Your folks said that I'm crazy! I don't give a damn, what they say. I'm your husband. You listen to me! Obey me! You love that grandmother more than you love me. Always talking about what she bought you. You better not put your foot out of this house, unless I'm with you. Taking food to the docks for them men. Soon they'll be putting their hands on you, that's if they haven't already. You got a husband now; you don't need to take nothing to the docks. Do you hear me?" Timmy stood glaring down at Zenna, who tearfully nodded. Zenna sat in shocked silence. A chill laid over her emotions. Zenna wished that she had something better. She thought about what Ma Sybil had said; bear with him dear, he'll come around. But now, she wondered. The smallest incident was magnified a thousand fold.

The next morning, before Timmy left for work, he nailed all the windows closed and padlocked both doors from the outside. Timmy left leaving a sonic trail of epithets. Zenna sat blinking away her tears. Zenna broke out the window around ten o' clock, and called her neighbor. They opened the window and ripped the lock off the back door. Her mind drifted off while her body remained at home. She was considering the situation politely. Zenna could see the vision in her brains. Timmy was so empty that he could fall forever within himself, reaching out for something, struggling, grasping, and nothing besides his shallow weightless bones would reach him.

Full of fear and hostility, Zenna decided that she really now, hated Timmy. Rufus was right, there was something confusing and neurotically wrong with Timmy. Suddenly Zenna's total physique had excruciating pain; her mind was so tired and befuddled, despite the efforts of her neighbor to revive it. There was nothing that could perk Zenna up. Her heart was really broken. The bright sunlight, the sweet smell of autumn flowers, and the chanting of the birds failed to restore her. What am I going to do? She thought. Zenna's mind floated back to when she was a girl at home and how happy she was then, and how kind and understanding Ma Sybil was. Zenna didn't visit Ma Sybil that day; she didn't want them to see her black eye.

Zenna thought to herself that they had to find a solution to their problem, all by themselves. At the time, Zenna couldn't see how. She laboriously carried on with her chores. When she had finished she sat down in the sunshine in the backyard, combing and brushing her long, heavy, black hair. Zenna knew that Timmy would come through the alley. He always did. It was a short cut for him. "Hi honey!" Zenna greeted Timmy when he opened the gate. Timmy was startled, his mouth flew open, and he began to stutter. His tongue was brimming over his words. The words crowding his throat, started flying in a blazing trail of epithets. " I thought I told you to stay in the house!" Timmy shouted. "How did you get out? Don't tell me, I know. That damn brother of yours let you out. Don't deny it. You are the hardest headed nigger I ever did see."

"Timmy you must be crazy." Zenna flipped up her prominent nose like a goat. "You know very well I'm not staying locked up in the house. No, Rufus didn't let me out. I haven't seen any of my family today. I did it all by myself."

"Oh yeah!" Timmy snapped. "Why are you still putting on those high blown airs, huh?" Timmy grabbed Zenna roughly by the hand, pulling her into the house. "You don't intend to obey me, I see." Timmy frowned his bucolic hand reaching for Zenna's hair. "I'll teach my wife a lesson!"

Timmy snatched Zenna to her knees, his muscular right arm swung high in the air, and with a metal pitcher grasped in the clenched brown fist; he clabbered Zenna over her head, face, and body. As Zenna uttered her appeal, she looked about in wild terror. When her cries were silent, Timmy tossed her on the bed. He went to the bathroom and washed off Zenna's blood.

Zenna laid there, not quite asleep and not awake. Lying motionless, just breathing the surface of the Savannah River. When Timmy had cleaned Zenna's blood from his hands, he strode to the bed and prodded Zenna in her ribs. She didn't flinch, she was too afraid. Timmy thinking that he had won his victory dished up a plate of food and put it on the table. As Timmy was about to sit down, nature called, and he plodded into the bathroom. Through slit eyes, Zenna stared at Timmy. She felt resentment and hatred. When she heard the water splashing into the toilet bowl, with some difficulty, she silently hobbled out of the backdoor. It slammed. The noise alarmed Timmy so much that the piss flew all over his pants and the floor. Timmy made an inspection to see just what the racket was about. "You still a hard headed nigger-bitch!" Timmy fumed, when he saw that the bed was empty. "Wait until I get my hands on you!" Timmy bellowed, staring at the empty bed. He glanced about, the floor, fussing all the while. "That's the hardest headed nigger I ever did see." When everything was in order Timmy sat and began to eat his dinner. He speared the meat viciously and bit it frightfully.

Zenna hobbled the four blocks and busted into Ma Sybil's door gasping for breath. Zenna was drenched in her blood. "Ma Sybil, Rufus," Zenna whispered. "Timmy! Timmy! Timmy, beat me! He locked me up in the house. I broke out…" Rufus took one look at Zenna, swung on his heels like an electric fan, not uttering a word. In a second, he was gone.

"Rufus! Wait! Wait! Wait Rufus, come back!" Ma Sybil called out, but it was already too late. Rufus dashed up to Timmy's front door, the big broken padlock stared him in the face. Timmy's neighbor pointed to the back of the house. Rufus raced to the alley. When he entered the backyard he snatched up an axe stuck into a block of wood. Rufus gave the door a powerful kick, almost detaching the door from its mooring.

Timmy sat eating. He made a surprise, but fruitless attempt to rise. The axe buried itself into a mass of flesh, almost severing Timmy's arm. Timmy slid to the floor. Rufus, without uttering a word, went out of the back door and stuck the axe into the stump of wood, and went home. While Rufus was walking home he began to think. What if the axe wasn't there? Rufus carried no weapon, ah well! It's over now, he thought.

Timmy staggered out of the house bloody, trying to push back a wave of malady. His owl eyes dilated with his lips fluttering, he yelled, "Help! Help! Help!" Timmy swiveled to the ground. A policeman walking his beat picked up Timmy's cries and went to his aid.

Timmy was hospitalized for a while. The torn ligaments to his right shoulder had to be stitched. The arm would be practically paralyzed for life. Timmy's boss, some co-workers, and his pastor visited him while he was in the hospital.

The sun's faint glaze was setting in the red, gold color making shadowy splashes on the porch. Ma Sybil bundled Zenna off in a taxi to a private doctor. Zenna had a broken arm and fractured ribs. Zenna felt as though she was standing off watching some drama happening to someone else. Her bosom was heavy with rage and indignation, and her blood was turning to ice water. Zenna was silent her eyes were glazed as if her thoughts were very far away. She was trembling uncontrollably, and had covered her face. Zenna had been married only three months; imagine that! Just three months in her whole life.

Zenna who had been thwarted by such a low hurdle, now realized the marriage was a mistake, and Rufus was right all along. Timmy was gone, gone from her forever. Time and events were obscured. Mingled together like an incubus that had no verity or motive. There were blank spots in her thoughts. Vague incidents rumbled along quickly, as if transported by a tornado. Rufus was arrested and his Uncle Albert posted bail. A few days later, Uncle Albert and Aunt Callie went to Timmy's flat and collected Zenna's belongings.

9

CHAPTER NINE

Timmy's mother Diana went to live with her brother Louis and his wife Sarah, after her mother died. Diana was eight years old. Louis Pettigrew and his wife Sarah were good to Diana, they sent her to school and she learned to read and write. When Diana was sixteen, she had glory in the bushes with another teenager. When Diana informed her lover she was pregnant, he panicked and left home.

When the baby was born, Diana named him Timmy. When Timmy was two months old, a group of fruit pickers came through their area, looking for workers. Some of Diana's friends were going to join the workforce. Diana convinced her brother and his wife to let her join them. They asked Diana, "What about the baby?" Diana was right on the mark; she said that Sarah could take care of Timmy. Diana pointed out, that Sarah cared for Timmy anyway and that she knew all about babies. Diana also said that she would send money to help out. She made a vow to the family that if anything happened to her they could claim Timmy as their own child. Diana left with the group, but she never wrote and she never went back. Many workers from Diana's area said they had seen Diana at various harvesting regions. Diana was quite alive and with a man, that she said was her husband.

Louis and Sarah loved Timmy as though he was their very own child, and he was christened Timmy Pettigrew. When they went out, Timmy was in his cradle on the wagon's floor between them. They were the only family that Timmy knew. When they worked in the fields, Uncle Louis had made a corral for Timmy, and Buzz, their dog guarded over Timmy while they worked.

CHAPTER NINE

When Timmy was old enough to go to school, the first day, Uncle Louis took him on a mule. Timmy's first day at school was a shock to him. His peers laughed at his coveralls shirt and shoes, which were all too large for him. Aunt Sarah said that children grew so fast, you should buy the clothes too big; so they can be used the next year. Timmy attended school only a few days. After that he stayed in the woods, played, and hunted rabbits and squirrels. He carried his sling shot every-where he went; and he was a good shot.

Timmy began to bring his bounty home, which made his uncle and aunt very proud of him. Uncle Louis and Aunt Sarah could not read nor write and it was sometime before they knew about Timmy skipping school. When they confronted Timmy about the guile, he cried and pleaded, and he told them how the children had made fun of his large clothes. Uncle Louis and Aunt Sarah weighed the situation and they gave in.

Timmy had worked in the fields since he was old enough to pull a handful of grass from around a plant. He liked the farm, and couldn't wait until he could handle a plow and make rows like Uncle Louis. The laborious work made Timmy strong, his hands, arms, legs, and chest were muscular, and soon he took charge of the farming. Timmy would leave home for work at sunrise and returned at sundown. He carried his food in a lard bucket, full with cornbread, syrup and butter. If the family had a good year, they had a slice of meat. As bare as they were, Uncle Louis was an independent farmer. They lived off what they made on the farm. For money they sold produce and livestock.

Many times Timmy and family sat to eat their food, engulfed in a pail of water, to keep the insets from the food. But the insects managed to get the food, anyway. Timmy observed Aunt Sarah sitting diligently, on the ground picking and brushing the ants off the food, and consuming it. Although Timmy loved the farm he didn't like the ants crawling over his food. When I'm a man I'll live in the city, then I'll buy an icebox, he thought.

CHAPTER NINE

Uncle Louis and Aunt Sarah didn't have much but what they had they shared, willingly with Timmy. The two-room shack was porous; an outdoor privy and a pump in the yard supplied them with water. When it rained containers had to be placed about the rooms to catch the water.

Aunt Sarah was a kind woman and just as clean. She was an interior decorator, of sorts. At Christmas, Aunt Sarah was busy decorating the house inside. She kinked the cracks with rags and paper to keep the wind out. Then she covered the whole walls with pages from Sears & Roebuck, Chicago Mail Order, Walter Field, and any other catalog she could find to cover the walls. It was quite decorative. On a windy night, the wind pushing against the rags and paper made music, as though a tune was being played on a harmonica. When Timmy heard the wind tune, he was seized with an irresistible desire to get up and Ball-the-Jack.

Uncle Louis and Aunt Sarah's shack was much better than most. Some of the shacks had big holes in them near the fireplaces. You could see the people inside and if time warranted you could shake hands through a crack.

Timmy had questioned his uncle and aunt about his birth mother many times. He asked them. "Why didn't my mother write? She could read and write. Why didn't she come to see us?" Timmy's uncle and aunt told him that they didn't know the reason, but there had to be one. Timmy said that he didn't like his birth mother, she didn't have a heart or soul and he hated her. Uncle Louis and Aunt Sarah said that Timmy should never say that about his mother, no matter how he felt about her. But that was the way Timmy felt.

Timmy Pettigre was illiterate, tall, strong and heavy-set. When Timmy went to Savannah from Waycross, Georgia, he was accustomed to hard work. Timmy was hired at a lumber-yard, loading trucks. He was thirty years old when he finally detached himself from his uncle and aunt. Timmy sent them money regularly and visited every Christmas. He never could get over the dislike he had for his mother. The feelings that he was a

CHAPTER NINE

cast-off by both parents, was a constant thought in his mind. When Timmy saw happiness and affection being displayed in Zenna's family it made his stomach churn. If his mother had stayed with him he would have learned to read and write, he thought. This point in Timmy's life kept grinding him down, until it almost consumed him.

10

CHAPTER TEN

After months of recuperating, Timmy, Zenna and Rufus' family and friends sat in Savannah's Criminal Courts and waited for justice. Rufus thought that Timmy, who had brutally beaten his sister and left an everlasting scar on her shoulder, would be sentenced. The judge was a small, short man with a razor shaped face and nose.

"Rufus Hannibal, IV, step forward." The court assistant said. The judge's face was cold and sullen. "Rufus, you acted like a mad man." The judge said crossly. "Yes, he did," thought Timmy. "A real mad man! I might not be able to use my arm again. Not like I used too, anyway. I hope he gets life." Timmy thought. Timmy's boss and some co-workers testified as character witnesses. "Timmy was the best damn nigger worker that I ever had." Timmy's boss stated.

Rufus, whistle clean and neat, wearing his best Swedish-blue suit; stood head bowed in humility. The magistrate continued, "Rufus! You shouldn't let your sisters problems enter into you. Let your sister take care of her own affairs. True, you would be outraged if you saw your sister bloody and hysterical. Any man would. But, after walking three blocks you had time to think and cool off. But you didn't. Rufus! You took the law into your own hands." The judge paused. His rat like eyes flowed over the small group of people who had accompanied Rufus as character witness. Ma Sybil, sat poised with her ears strained.

The judge took from the stack of judgments that was before him. He puckered his brow and cast a fleeting glance in Timmy's direction. Then the judge spoke. "Rufus Hannibal, IV, due to your youth, your spotless record, and your family background." The judge paused. "You will not be sentenced to the maximum of the law." Rufus' group felt light inside and smiled within themselves. That brut Timmy is going to get what he deserves, they thought.

At that moment, everything was either, happening to fast or too slow. Then they heard it. A sound like a sharp crack of lightening. "Rufus Hannibal, IV, I hereby sentence you to one year on the Georgia Chain Gang, with time off with good behavior." Rufus was poker faced but his head and face were burning. He felt as though blood was dripping from his eyes. Rufus sensed that the entire world's vastness and its ability to change, was cut off from him by imperceptible curtain. The world was rearing and tearing under his feet. He felt that such a verdict was inhuman.

Zenna was uncontrollable. Her wail was deafening and the fever of the people rose intensely. "Silence!" Yelled the judge. "Or I'll have the bailiff clear the courtroom." All the noise died away in the room and the low, nocturnal lackluster tone of voices subsided, inaudible in the silence.

CHAPTER TEN

It was only, the misfortunes and heartaches, through the years that kept Ma Sybil from fainting. Ma Sybil pondered, her good son, young and handsome Rufus was now a fugitive on the chain gang. Rufus had only tried to protect his family, Ma Sybil thought.

Rufus was indicted for assault with a deadly weapon. His family was baffled and enraged. At that moment Rufus hated all society, and he didn't give a damn anymore. How dare the judge sentence him? Didn't Timmy, that big ape of a bastard damage his sister's arm? Fuck Timmy's arm! What about his sister's arm and his family's feelings? Doesn't that count? Rufus thought.

Timmy's deep set eyes were dancing. Not knowing what his fate would be, cocked his head to one side and waited. The magistrate's rat like eyes glittered behind his glasses. "Timmy Pettigrew!" The judge called out, his voice full and it crescened, "Timmy! You stay away from your wife. Unless your wife decides to reconciliation, don't go near her! If you do, and you come into my court again, I will throw the book at you. Do you understand?"

"Yes sir, your honor." Timmy spoke, his head looping up and down like a hungry bird picking up worms. "I am never going near them people." "Timmy Pettigrew! You may go now." The judge said, as he closed the file. "Next case!"

Ma Sybil family and friends watched Rufus, away. They also saw Timmy's smug face beaming inside for his good fortune. Timmy strutted nonchalantly out of the courtroom. His arm was in a sling, Zenna's arm was also in a sling. Zenna dabbed at her eyes with her handkerchief, while being supported to the street by Ma Sybil and family. Zenna was hysterical, "Hush child!" Ma Sybil consoled. "Justice don't always come as we expect." Ma Sybil uttered.

Ma Sybil was like a healthy, sheltering, Giant Redwood Tree, in the California desert, with its long life and leaves that rustled in the wind. A tree that was washed by rain, sun, and earthquakes, but still it gleamed in the sunlight. Ma Sybil was like that tree that blossomed and bore fruits in spite of all the earthquakes that beat and tried to break it.

Rufus was packed off in the Black Mariah, full with other prisoners. Among the convicts was Craig Baker. Rufus and Craig were shackled together. Craig, the same age as Rufus, lives with his mother, a domestic worker. They lived in a three room flat above a fish store. Craig's father had died when he was ten years old. Craig was tall, lanky, and bright eyed. He had an older sister, who lived in New York City. Craig and Rufus were among older men who smelled of death. Men who were found guilty of murder, rape, and burglary.

Craig Baker helped out in all kinds of odd jobs. His mother's boss gave Craig extra work, cutting the grass and simonizing the car. Since Craig was good at mathematics, the boss encourage him to continue his education. One day after Craig finished cleaning up his boss' black Cadillac, his eyes feasted on the splendid job he had done. He was so pleased, that he got the urge to go for a drive. Why not? He thought. No one will know.

White people have everything and we niggers have nothing. I will sport this baby for a while, and people will think it's mine.

It was a pleasant, early October day. The delightful breeze wandered over the earth, gently rustling the leaves. Craig reflected on picking up his girlfriend and taking her for a drive. He entered an intersection, the light changed quickly, but Craig was slow to take off. The big Mack truck behind him was too fast and collided with the Cadillac. The impact pushed the back of the Cadillac almost into the front seat. Craig wasn't physically hurt but his feelings were. He was terribly frightened, even dazed. Craig fled the scene.

Craig's mother was horrified about the accident, and her boss pressing charges. She tried to persuade her boss not to have Craig arrested. She told her boss that she would pay off the debt, no matter how long it took. The boss told Craig's mother, that he wasn't being mean, because he had Craig arrested. But, Craig must be taught a lesson. If Craig was allowed to get away with this incident, perhaps he would try something else, which might be more disastrous.

Craig's mother tearfully called her daughter in New York and related the whole episode to her. "Mother, don't be so upset." Her daughter said. "There is some truth in what your boss said. When Craig's sentence is commuted, I will send for him. I am sure that he can get a job on the docks where my husband works."

Craig was sentenced to one year on the chain gang and time off for good behavior, same as Rufus.

Rufus never had a real male friend and he was grateful for Craig's friendship. Rufus and Craig were eager to get out and start a new life. Both their time on the chain gang was easy. They were sent to the Warden's home to help his wife with household chores and gardening. They were also good with the children. There was one thing they would not do and that was piggy back rides. Rufus claiming that he had a bad back from lifting heavy crates at the produce market. Rufus and Craig were model prisoners and were out in six months.

Both Rufus and Craig vowed never to be locked up again. They realized that living a lawless life style wasn't the life to live. Seldom did anyone living that style rise above the station of a low life, having sunk to the very depth of a four-footed animal.

Ma Sybil's words encourage Rufus to be a good detainee. Zenna also pledged to visit Rufus every guest day. As she blamed herself for Rufus' incarceration. Zenna took sweets, cigarettes, and a book, "House of the Dead", by Dostoyevsky. Rufus' friend, Margie supported Rufus while he was away.

Craig's mother also was on hand with gifts and her support for her son. After work Rufus and Craig rushed to their bunks and read the material that was brought to them. Rufus and Craig stood in a cesspool; trying to reach out in space for the thing we call life.

CHAPTER TEN

Rufus and Craig, who had never been away from their families, and now on the chain gang, was a hideous nightmare for them. They attested not to have such an experience again. After they had read their material they perceived that under a slight different surface, the years were precisely what they had been. Mankind was still divided into species; the few who had continuity in their souls, and the many who had none. Rufus and Craig always talked about the past and hopes for the future. There was always laughter between them. When their time was up, they drew in a deep breath of fresh air, cleaning their lungs of the loathsome stench of prison.

Rufus and Craig, homebound, descended form the bus and shook hands like veterans. They smiled and looked deep into each others eyes and declared that from then on, they would try to keep away from negative people. Rufus spoke softly, "I'll avoid negative people who attempt to bring me down to their level of thinking." Rufus released Craig's hand and proudly strolled off. Craig said, 'Same thing here," as they waved to each other and parted company. Rufus went back to Yamacraw and Craig to Gwinnett Street.

Craig's sister had made the necessary preparation for him to leave for New York, immediately. Craig had pledge to Rufus that he would write him as soon as he was established and if Rufus wanted to come to New York, he would send for him and wire him a ticket. Rufus appreciated the favor and though maybe, someday, he would accept the challenge, but not as long as Ma Sybil was alive.

11

CHAPTER ELEVEN

Rufus was welcomed home. Everything was much the same as when he left. Rufus and Margie took up where they left off. Although, Zenna and Timmy hadn't had any communication, Ma Sybil and family thought that it would be best that Zenna leave Savannah, to seek a new life elsewhere. Ma Sybil knew that Zenna wasn't going back to Timmy. "Zenna was still young and a lovely person." Ma Sybil said. So, when Ma Sybil's sister Julia and her husband Oscar Grant in Jacksonville, Florida visited them, Ma Sybil and the family discussed the matter. Uncle Oscar and Aunt Julia were very pleased to have Zenna living with them. It seemed ages since their own children had left home.

Aunt Julia was a salad maker at a prominent hotel. The morning that Aunt Julia took Zenna with her to the job, for a tour, Aunt Julia stopped at a small candy store. She had to put her bolita numbers in. Sam Dorkins, the storeowner, was tall, with tan smooth skin and good looking. He displayed curly brown hair rolled tight, like dark wild cherries. At first sight, Sam was smitten with Zenna. Sam was 28, but looked 20, was macho towards women. He was stylish and a real fashion plate. He was a big wheel, black number in Jacksonville. Sam owned the small shop, a four-room cottage that was perched on one acre of land, and he drove a new shiny Cadillac.

"Who's this pretty, young lady you have with you, Miss Julia?" Sam asked. His gold plated teeth and pink gums concealing his extra years and causing him to look almost boyish.

"This is Zenna Pettigrew, my great niece from Savannah, Georgia.' Aunt Julia introduced. "Zenna is here looking for work and a good husband." Julia chuckled.

"What kind of work she does?" Sam inquired anxiously. "Maybe, I can help put there. I know many people."

"Well, Zenna finished high school." Aunt Julia replied proudly. "She can type write and keep books. Lordy! She isn't a dummy like me. Where can a black woman find that kind of work around here? So, I'm taking Zenna to the hotel where I work to care for two young children."

"Well, if Zenna is good at figures," Sam ventured, "maybe I can help. I need someone who can keep books and look after the store too. I'm looking for a good wife, just like Zenna." Zenna blushed at the forward remarks.

"Thanks a million!" Aunt Julia said. "But we'll make the day, since the woman is expecting Zenna. Come to the house tonight and we will discuss it.' When they walked a few blocks,

Zenna tugged at Aunt Julia's arm. "Does Sam read and write?" Zenna asked almost in a whisper.

"Of course, Sam can read and write." Aunt Julia spoke out, eyeing Zenna sheepishly. "Why do you ask child?" At that moment Aunt Julia had forgotten about Timmy's ignorance.

"My husband Timmy couldn't read or write," Zenna explained. "I don't want another illiterate man."

"You don't have to worry about Sam, honey." Aunt Julia stated. "Sam's quite a figure head. He does need someone who's honest, to help out in the store. He had many clerks in the store, but I heard that they stole everything they could. Sam doesn't trust anyone and the store is closed most of the time."

Later that night, Aunt Julia and Uncle Oscar discussed whether Zenna should work for Sam Dorkins. Of course, Sam was a number's man; everyone knew that. Sam was generous. He helped the needy and he gave large contributions to the church; even though he didn't belong to any church. Sam was sought after; and many women tried to snare him.

CHAPTER ELEVEN

When Sam arrived that night, Uncle Oscar spoke up. "Sam! If your intentions are good, it's alright for Zenna to work for you." Aunt Julia bowed her head in agreement.

"In the mean time," Uncle Oscar stated between coughs and wheezing, "we are church people and we don't want Zenna sleeping out all night." Uncle Oscar had high principles and scruples; he wasn't about to let Sam Dorkins forget that. He didn't care if Sam was a big shot number's man.

"You don't have to worry about that." Sam informed. "Zenna won't stay out all night with me until we are married. You can count on that." Sam charmed. The next day, Zenna started to work for Sam Dorkins, her future husband.

Uncle Oscar started out was a fourth cook on the L&N Railroad. He met his wife, Julia, on one of his rums. Julia was on her way to Jacksonville, Florida to relatives in search for work. They were both young and their courtship developed into marriage and two children. Oscar Grant worked up to steward in the diner. In his pear shaped kitchen his tall, thin frame, brown face with piercing eyes, peeped through the hole in the serving window. Uncle Oscar was a hard boiled, crocodile, the waiters called him. The cooks and waiters were all up a tree when Oscar bellowed through the small serving window. "Hey! You bird-brains, drag-ass niggers! What's this order doing here? Uncle Oscar's shinny sweaty face and his pea eyes were dancing behind his steam up glasses. He didn't dare to move from his tracks, until he dried his sweaty glasses on a large handkerchief that he always carried for that purpose. When the glasses were back on his eyes, with authority the bellowing started all over again.

Uncle Oscar's staff called him Simon Legree. But after the rush and the mop-up was finished, Uncle Oscar was relaxed. He and crew ate, drank, and laughed together.

Uncle Oscar was a good man and had a heart of gold. He always gave the married men extra to take home. Chicken liver, wings, gizzards, necks, hams, a whole chicken, and sometimes a small turkey found its way to the home of married men. "Take this to the missy." Uncle Oscar would say.

When mealtime was busy, Uncle Oscar went into his act. "You drag-ass niggers don't think that you're going to run me up a tree?" Uncle Oscar declared, glaring about to see if anyone would challenge him. Uncle Oscar had his ways about him. He would pile the whip of muteness by taking his time to answer any questions. When he thought he had been insulted, he took off his glasses and wiped his sweaty brow. "What is that supposed to mean?" He would exclaim.

When Zenna started to work for Sam Dorkins there were only a few articles on the shelves. It was just a place for numbers. Zenna persuaded Sam to fully stock the store. Since she would be there every day, all day, except Sundays. Sam gave Zenna permission to stock the store as she liked. After the store was stocked, it began to thrive. Everyone liked Zenna; she was friendly, pretty, kind, helpful, and considerate. Sam was very proud of Zenna; her salary was five dollars a week.

"Zenna! You got these people eating out of your hand.
How do you do it? Some of these people never put their foot into
this store, before now. They come in everyday. I mean the
snooty kind. Of course, their airs never bothered me. All I'm in-
terested in is making money."

12

CHAPTER TWELVE

Zenna and Sam jointed Aunt Julia's church. Sam wanted to prove to everyone that he was a worthy person. He really did love Zenna. She was new blood in his life. It seemed as though Sam had been waiting for Zenna all those years.

Two years after Timmy was wounded with an axe, he received a wire that his Uncle Louis Pettigrew had died from lung sickness and old age. Timmy went home immediately. Shortly after Timmy arrived home, Aunt Sarah had a stroke. The shock was too much for her.

Before the doctor left the house, Aunt Sarah died from a heart attack. Timmy was at a loss. No one loved him now, and everyone he lived was gone. He sold the few livestock Uncle Louis left alone with some of Aunt Sarah's fancy quilts; and used the little money he had to purchase lumber for two coffins. Timmy and some of the deacons from the church stayed up most of the night to finish building the two boxes. Timmy buried his loved ones side by side.

Timmy too back to Savannah, few momentous from the people he knew loved him and that he loved him. He was a sad and broken man. He wasn't the same after the axe attack. His boss gave him work around the place, whatever he could handle. Timmy didn't visit the church anymore. His pastor and members visited him; and encourage him to come back to church. "When I feel better". He told them.

Timmy just worked and went home and stayed there. One morning, he didn't show up to work. Around ten o'clock, the boss sent a worker to check on him. When the coworker got no response, the door was forced opened. There Timmy laid on the bed, dead; rigormortis had already set in.

CHAPTER TWELVE

When Zenna heard Timmy was dead, she told Sam.
Zenna and Sam immediately began to make plans for their wedding. Zenna though that she had met the perfect man for a husband. Sam was intelligent, handsome, ambitious, and loving. Everything a woman wanted in a good husband. Sam and Zenna had a quiet wedding at Aunt Julia's house. After they were settled, they took part in the community activities. Sam and Zenna were beginning to have a rich and full life. A year later, they drove to Savannah to visit Ma Sybil and the family. Everyone was glad to see Zenna and her husband. They said that Zenna had found her man at last. Every holiday, Zenna remembered her family with gifts.

In the coming years, Sam and Zenna were blissful. They enlarged the store and added four-rooms to the house. Zenna decorated and landscaped the whole scenery. This is how to live and be happy, Zenna thought.

Zenna's first miscarriage left her very ill, she lost weight and very weak. After the second miscarriage, Zenna's doctor advised her not to try again. It was too dangerous. Zenna and Sam were very disappointed.

Zenna wanted so much to have a baby. She never forgot the first time she held Kay, Rena Mae's baby. Kay was so warm, small, and cute. Zenna said that when she married, she was going to have children. Zenna wanted to nurture her children, and have a clean, safe home for them. Maybe, someday they would adopt; if not, they still had each other to love.

13

CHAPTER THIRTEEN

One morning when Rufus awoke, he didn't hear the tinkling of utensils in the kitchen. He got up and went to Ma Sybil's room and knocked on the door. There was no response. Rufus opened the door, "Ma Sybil, are you all right?" he asked softly from the doorway. Still, there was no answer. Rufus sucked in a deep breath and edged forward. Ma Sybil had just passed her seventy-fifth birthday. When Rufus reached the bed, his heart skipped wildly as he peered down at his grandmother. Maybe she's dead, the thought. Panicked, Rufus shook uncontrollably. He bent forward and saw Ma Sybil struggling to breathe. Ma Sybil's clogged chest made her choke for air. Rufus was straining toward the fragile, thin body as if to give it life.

Ma Sybil's wrinkled face and arms were somewhat aged, as

though aged overnight. Over the knuckled bones, the outline of

veins stood out, blue and vertical. "Ma Sybil! Can you hear me?

Are you all right?" Rufus asked again in a voice that quivered

with dread. There was still no visible response. Ma Sybil had

been ailing for sometime from bronchitis and arthritis. She was

up and about; she refused to give in to her condition. Rufus was

breathless, weightless, and some worry lines loomed around his

lips and eyes. Ma Sybil moved uneasily and with some agitation.

"Is that you Rufus?" The voice was so feeble with fatigue; it was

barely audible.

"Yes Mama, its me." Rufus spoke clutching Ma Sybil's

hand. "What time is it?" Rufus informed Ma Sybil. "Are you all

right, Ma Sybil?" Rufus inquired. "Sure, I'm fine." Ma Sybil

spoke faintly. "Don't fret so much. I'll be okay. The doctor will

be here soon". Rufus assured Ma Sybil. With some effort, Ma

Sybil opened her eyes as wide as she could. She saw her only grandson weeping; the child whom she loved most. Ma Sybil's

throat was like a tree whose roots had crossed and smothered

one another. You could hear Ma Sybil speaking against an

enormous mass in her throat. Ma Sybil's chest caused the breath

to emerge in squirts.

"The doctor will be here soon and he will make you bet-

ter." Rufus confided to Ma Sybil, as he bent down and kissed her

lined cheek with tenderness. He then pulled the cover up around

her wasted shoulders, protectively.

"No Rufus! It's too late," Ma Sybil remarked, "I've had a

good life, trying, but good and a very happy life, too. I had the

pleasure bringing up my children and my grandchildren. I held

my great-grandchild. Take care of Lulu; she's the only one who

isn't grown yet. Rufus, be the man I know you'll be. Always

look out for your sisters". Yes, Ma Sybil. You know that I will

do that". Rufus said softly.

"Rufus! Take the key from my neck," Ma Sybil in-

structed. "Under my bed is a small chest. The instructions in the box will tell you what to do. There's also some money in the post office, give Albert, Callie, Zenna, and Rena Mae one hundred dollars a piece. The rest you keep for yourself and Lulu." Rufus did as he was told. He sat on the bed, took Ma Sybil's small hands into his and gently rubbed them.

"Ma Sybil, don't fret." Rufus expressed. "The doctor will make you feel better." With closed eyes, Rufus stumbled out of the room to open the door for Uncle Albert and Aunt Callie. Rena Mae and the doctor reached Ma Sybil's house at the same time. Uncle Albert led Rufus from Ma Sybil's room so that the doctor could attend to her. Only Uncle Albert remained in the room. The doctor gave Ma Sybil medication to ease her breathing.

"The medicine will make you rest." The doctor stated. "You mother won't last through the night." The medic whispered to Uncle Albert. "No need to take her to the hospital. If you have other family, better get in touch with them," the doctor said.

CHAPTER THIRTEEN

After the doctor left, the family entered Ma Sybil's room. The coughing had somewhat abated. Ma Sybil opened her eyes and looked about. "Where is Zenna? I want to see her before I go."

"Zenna and the rest of the family are on their way." Uncle Albert spoke. Around four o'clock that day, Zenna and the family arrived from Jacksonville, Florida. Zenna was the first to dash from the car. Her face was wet with tears.

"Ma Sybil! Please don't leave me!" Zenna pleaded, pressing her small hand and kissing her fevered brow.

"Zenna! Is that you?" Ma Sybil asked. "I was waiting for you. I knew that you would come." Aunt Julia squeezed in and tool hold of Ma Sybil's hand. "Sylvia! Do you know who I am?" "Yes, I know you. You are my sister, Julia". Ma Sybil spoke. "You think I have lost my wits. Don't fret now! I will be all right. I'm going where there won't be any sorrow and no hurt."

Ma Sybil's breathing was getting laborious. The men stood mute, as the women touch some parts of Ma Sybil's body.

"Rena Mae! How is the baby? Take good care of my great-grandchild."

"I'll do my best." Rena Mae stated, tears flowing down her face. Rena Mae was really sad about loosing her grandmother. Although they didn't always see eye to eye, she loved her grandmother and wanted her around. Ma Sybil was the best cook in the world, Rena Mae thought.

"I know that Rufus will look after Lulu." Ma Sybil whispered. After soft prayers and melodious singing, Ma Sybil closed her eyes, stretched out full-length and passed away.

The air in the garden was heavy with sea peas and honeysuckle blossoms. Ma Sybil died in the same bed where her husband died and her two children was born.

Rufus with wet eyes went into his room, as he stood by the window and said, "How do we see death, not as an evil spirit, but as a liberator to free one who is no longer able to sustain itself, in any form. Oh death, where is thy sting; oh grave, where is thy victory? Rest Ma Sybil; the sting hurts deeply, but the victory is peace and tranquility. She was a great woman who had touched so many people." Inside, Rufus was still shrinking from the power of death.

Lulu, the youngest at the time, was the closest to Ma Sybil. She dogged Ma Sybil's every trail. When Ma Sybil passed, Lulu turned gray, but said nothing. She slipped away to the backyard to converse with herself. Lulu sat, swinging under the Chinaberry Tree. She swung and cried silently.

Uncle Albert and Rufus made the funeral arrangements, while the family, a host of friends, and church members paid their respects to Ma Sybil. Steele, the undertaker, dressed the body. They had never done a nicer job. The Wake was held at the house where Ma Sybil had lived since Phillip Anderson carried over the threshold. The church was packed like long stem matches in a box. Ma Sybil's funeral was held at the church where her husband, Phillip, daughter Agnes, and granddaughter Zenna first marriage was held. The Pastor was proudly and clearly enjoying himself with his jerky, lengthy ceremony.

Rufus' mind was straying on other unrelated topics. What kind of arrangements he could make with Uncle Albert and Aunt Callie, to keep Lulu until he could send for her? How much money he would get for the house? How soon will it take before he'll leave for New York?

The funeral procession traveled to Laurel Cemetery. Ma Sybil was buried beside her husband, Phillip, and her daughter, Agnes, was on the other side. The former headstone seemed to have sunken a few inches. For the first time in Rufus' life, he knew the he was finished with Yamacraw.

14

CHAPTER FOURTEEN

At Margie's flat, the first Saturday night after Ma
Sybil's funeral, suddenly, the Rock Cola stopped playing and the
house was thrown into pitch darkness. Free electric lights had
ended in Margie's apartment. Rufus was late reaching Margie's
address that night. There was so much to do after Ma Sybil's
death. There wasn't any light in the hall. Margie was sitting in
the dark, crying.

"What happened?" Rufus asked after stumbling over a
piece of furniture. "Somebody turned me in." Margie uttered silently, wiping her tears. "Now I'm ruined. I can't make any
money!"

"Well, don't carry on so." Rufus tried to encourage Margie. "Monday morning you go to the light company and tell them that the lights was on when you moved into the flat and now you're willing to pay for the electricity that you will be using. I will go with you, but I won't go inside".

"Okay." Margie said, trusting Rufus' idea. He had lived in the city all his life and he knew about city things. Rufus and Margie spent the quiet two nights together, in the darkness.

Monday morning, Margie and Rufus dressed in their best apparel and headed downtown to get accommodation for the light company. When Margie arrived at the light company, the doors had just opened.

Margie went in and explained to the light company about the lights, that they were on when she rented the house, and she thought that the service went with the rent. The company didn't buy Margie's story.

"Well, your landlord should have told you that the lights did not go with the rent. You know it had been quite a bit of pilfering of our company lately. When we discover a situation as yours and there are other; we don't service them, not even for money."

Margie emerged from the office in tears. "They refused to turn the lights on." Margie related to Rufus. "Now, I'm really ruined." Margie still sniffling, said "how can I carry on without lights?"

"Don't worry." Rufus consoled. Suddenly his brain opened up. "Why don't you take our house?" You could let the lights stay in Grandpa Phillip's name. Just pay the bill. Nobody will know about it, but you and me."

"Your house!" Margie was alarmed, "What will I do with that big house? It had eight bedrooms and besides, your house is in Yamacraw. I will loose all my customers."

"That's all the better." Rufus assured Margie. "The bigger the house, the bigger the business. You will acquire other customers. In Yamacraw, you will make more money because you would catch the dock workers before they get uptown. You could make the place something big. I know you could. Sorry that I won't be around to help you. You know how I feel about this town. I am leaving for New York, as soon as I can get things settled. Why don't you buy the house? Pay some money down and the rest like rent. Someday, the house will be yours; your home. You can have the furniture. Uncle Albert's house is full. He might want a piece or so, you won't mind that; and you could sell your furniture."

"Well, I guess I have no choice." Margie dried her eyes.

"Oh, you have a choice." Rufus continued. "There are plenty of empty houses around. If you don't want to buy or rent our house, then rent another house. I will have the lights turned on in my name or whoever you wish to do so".

"You are so right." Margie stated, squeezing Rufus' hand. "On second thought, I will take your house. It is some truth to what you said about catching the dock workers before they get uptown."

"Well, if you are going to buy the house, you've have to do it legally." Rufus pointed out. "You must have a lawyer. I will get in touch with Uncle Albert, Zenna, and Rena Mae so they can sign off. Within a month, all the house business should be straightened out. We will rest today, but tomorrow, we will move your things in."

Paying light bills in the ghetto of Savannah and in some better section as well, during The Depression time was practically nile. When a tenant moved form an apartment, the light company removed the registering meter and closed the receptacle. Two wires were left unattached. Need always provided a way for the less fortunate. A man who called himself "Big Red" would go around, wherever a new tenant engaged a flat, and make the necessary connection for two dollars.

Those were perilous times. Tenants who were tardy with their rent would find their apartments emptied by their landlords, who used strong men that would work for two dollars. Weak men were jostled aside while the strong men rushed into the flat and dumped all the household articles onto the sidewalk. The landlord then secured the door with a heavy padlock and went his way. In the meantime, the evictee carried their belongings to the nearest empty house and moved in. by doing this they saved a dollar, which would keep them eating for a week. A nickel would feed a family of five a whole day, a penny worth of crack rice, a penny neck bones, a penny cornmeal, kool-aid, and a penny worth of coal oil.

Many houses in Yamacraw stood as shells. Chilly weather and no money to obtain fuel for the fireplaces; numerous houses were stripped for wood. Some property owners allowed the tenants to stay in their buildings if they got any money at all.

After Rufus had arranged his affairs, he deposited Lulu to Uncle Albert and Aunt Callie. Rufus shooed the dust of Yamacraw forever from his soul.

In the sky hung a clearly, defined fluffy cloud. From the clouds fell trickles of rain, broken with the morning rainbow hue and falling the train flying over the rails. Rufus had tried to convince Margie to come with him to New York, bust she refused. Her mother was the reason. She wanted to be near her should anything happen. Margie's father was a good man for the children, but he was mean to her mother and he abused her.

Rufus left Margie's house, his old home since was six years old. He took a taxi to the train station with his dark blue suitcase were straining under his belt. Here it is! The L & N, backed into Savannah's Union Station. During The Depression, the train was belching out huge pillows of steam and smoke. The conductor was getting ready to head north.

Rufus was conspicuously dressed; he wore a light blue suit with large stripes. A Cab Callaway watch chain dangled almost to his knees. Most of the better-dressed country young men, at that time tried to mimic Cab's mode of dressing. Rufus wore a wide brim hat with a light blue feather pulled down over his ears. The long feather quivered in the breeze and his black narrow toe shoes, too large for his feet, slapped the ground.

Rufus embarked from the train; the crisp fall air stung his nostril and he twitched his nose like a rabbit. "Rufus! Over here!" called Rufus' good friend, Craig Baker. Rufus swung on his heels and they pumped hands. Craig and Rufus poked one another in the ribs as they clicked their teeth. They eyed each other and broke into a big laugh. Craig's eyes picked up the wrinkled, cheap suit that Rufus was wearing. Craig wondered how he could get Rufus into his flat before anyone he knew saw them. "Leave the bags man." Craig echoed. "We will pick them up tomorrow. You can wear some of my clothes. We wear the same size, anyway." A little episode they would laugh about years later. "All right." Rufus agreed, glad to be with his one true friend again. Craig hailed a cab and directed him to a Co-vent Avenue address. Mildred, Craig's wife that's seven months pregnant, greeted Rufus warmly. Craig outfitted Rufus in his latest New York fashions. They went out to dinner and Craig showed Rufus Harlem. Rufus watched the black people strutting their stuff. He saw destiny working, filling thousands of soulful eyes with resignation to live and searching to encompass what yoked them down. In this section of New York, Rufus saw Ya-macraw. NO! NO! 125th Street wasn't for Rufus; visit there, yes, but live there, never. Rufus knew that environment was more

more intimated with Rena Mae's world. She swiveled off at a different angle.

After dinner and sight seeing, they visited the Apollo Theater and that night was 'Amateur Night'. Rufus enjoyed the show and he hardly laugh when 'Puerto Rico' came out to shoo away the unfortunate performer from the stage. Rufus was fascinated and excited with New York. He hadn't seen anything like it.

Rufus had a wonderful first day in New York. The next day, Rufus, alone, toured the whole city via subway for a nickel. Craig had told Rufus how he could ride the trains and how to use the crossover to go in different directions.

When the week was up, Rufus had learned to travel the five boroughs of New York by subway. Rufus' second week in New York, Craig took him to his job and he was hired as a longshoreman. Rufus was fortunate to be working with Craig. Rufus was a good worker and got along with his coworker. Rufus kept Uncle Albert and the rest of the family posted concerning his job, New York, and about himself.

When Rufus was in New York for six months, he sent for Lulu. He rented a flat in the same building where Craig lived. Rufus had furnished the two-bedroom apartment and all was in readiness for Lulu. Lulu was sweet, clean, and very subtle. She was glad to be united with her brother and his friend. Lulu supervised the flat and was very excited with New York, its beauty, gaiety, and the advancement for blacks.

Lulu enrolled in Madam C. J. Walker's Beauty School. She was an excellent student and finished her course with honors. While learning her craft at Madam Walker, Lulu met Harold Jones, an auditor for the school. Harold auditioned the books once a week. He was a New Yorker, young, handsome, and six feet tall. Harold fell in love with Lulu at first sight and Lulu's sensors were feathery. Harold was born with a clubfoot, one leg shorter than the other was and he tipped up on his toes as he walked. Harold's schoolmates nicknamed him Tip. The name stuck with the owlish eyed, pinch mouth all through his life. He was an only child. His mother worked in a boutique shop. Harold dressed very fashionable and he was very popular wherever he was known.

Lulu kept in touch with Rena Mae. She told her how beautiful New York was. She also informed her that black people in New York didn't ride in the back of buses or trains; they didn't say yes maam, unless they wanted to. Rena Mae was quite excited about all the charm displayed in Lulu's letters and, too, was a little lonesome for her family. Rena Mae started saving up money for a one-way ticket to New York. When Lulu told Rufus that Rena Mae was coming to New York to live, he cringed. "What does she want to come here for?" He thought. "Zenna is in Jacksonville, Florida which is much closer to Savannah, why doesn't she go there? Zenna was grown and married and Rena Mae was also grown and had a child. She gave the child away. He had Lulu to care for and he wanted to see her married to a good man." Rufus thought. Rena Mae had always made a big mess and left it for somebody else to clean up. She too was his sister and his mother and Ma Sybil said before they died, 'always look after your sisters, Rufus'.

225

THE CROSSING OF YAMACRAW

When time was near for Rena Mae to come to New York, Rufus rented a large front room with cooking privileges. The room was located on 126th Street, right behind the Apollo Theater. Rufus paid for a month and that made the short, stout, black, wrinkled, landlady smile from ear to ear showing some missing front teeth. Rufus knew his sister Rene Mae and wasn't going to have her around messing up everybody's lives.

The evening that Rena Mae arrived, the air was high with intensity. Lulu had prepared a delectable, healthy dinner, and after the feast was over Rena Mae acquainted them concerning the latest happenings in Savannah. The next day, Lulu escorted Rene Mae to her new abode. Rena Mae was very pleased indeed about the arrangement. She was not going to have Rufus bossing her around, she thought. From St. Nickolas Avenue to Fifth Avenue, on 125th Street, Rena Mae frequently met someone who was from Yamacraw; 'from down home, Rena Mae called it.

The air was cordial for Rena Mae, within a week she found a soul mate for her bed and he shared her room. His name

CHAPTER FOURTEEN

was Jed Mack, tall, good looking, older man, who sold insurance during the day and worked as a waiter at night. After Rena Mae's illness while she lived in Savannah, she didn't have the large protruding, juicy looking but as before. "My big hips, I wished I still had them." Rena Mae would say. Rena Mae was now a six o'clock model with warm, light brown, attractive flesh. Men chased after Rena Mae like children in a field with butterflies.

15

CHAPTER FIFTEEN

Harold Jones was five years older than Lulu. Rufus and Lulu didn't mind that because Harold was intelligent and he had drive. When Lulu had finished her beauty course, she and Harold were married. Six months after they were married, with Harold's help, Lulu opened a four-chair beauty parlor. Lulu's adeptness in the air of beautification soon gratified her with a very lucrative business. Some years later, Harold and Lulu were blessed with a healthy and beautiful daughter. They named her Mitzy and added much happiness to an already compatible home.

CHAPTER FIFTEEN

With Lulu, now married, Rufus gave his own life a long serious thought. He always wanted a woman with dignity, intelligence, quality, a sense of pride and charm, like Ma Sybil. Since Rufus hadn't finished high school, he didn't think he would find such a woman. He wanted a woman who knew how to do much more than just rattle pots and pans. He had visualized a lady with grace and poise, who would illuminate his home and radiate a light in the darkest corners. Rufus wanted to make his wife happy, and to appreciate her. He wanted to consider his wife the highest of honor and the greatest of joy to have in his home. Rufus would dedicate himself to her body and soul, forever. He had met a few women in New York, but none to his liking. Then Rufus' mind swung back to Margie and the good times they had together. Rufus still had Margie in his system, but knew Margie wasn't going to leave Savannah; and he wasn't going to leave New York.

Rufus also knew that Margie liked her new home. The house he was brought up in. it gave him pleasure to know that the house was being cared for. Rufus also knew Margie's way of life and she wasn't going to change. Rufus was filled to the brim with fragmentary, fortuitous, recollection of Margie; the woman whose stamp, at various times had crossed his path. Rufus wrote Margie a letter, stating that he was getting married soon as he met the proper person. He asked Margie to write back and say whether she wanted to be that person.

Margie wrote back and said as much as she wanted to be with him, she couldn't. She did not want to leave Savannah be-cause her mother was still alive. Her father was sometimes cruel to her mother. He was a good father, as he protected his children and home, but he had broken her mother's nose and arm in the past. So, she wanted to be close to home, just in case something happened to her mother.

At Margie's first flat, Rufus had brushed with wealthy white and black men of the sporting world. They had cross talked and laughed to the rich liquor, and the recorded music of Duke Ellington's "Black and Tan Fancy", "Sophisticated Lady", and Louis Armstrong's "I'll Be Glad When You're Dead, You Rascal You"; and Rufus was delighted with Louie blowing his tunes. Many beautiful young women and men hung out at Margie's new place for drinks and whatever else that came their way for a snare. Some of the black people at Margie's suite was so fair that they would make Jew's and Latin's look like Nubbians beside them. Well to do blacks of consequence and certain groups of wealthy whites, met and mingled freely, naturally, for amusement in flats and roadhouses. At times, there were a few rich, beautiful white women, who were seeking new interests in their dull stagnate world. The atmosphere was intense and overcharge with currents of personal reaction. It was rumored that orgies were held on certain nights.

Margie had no call girls, but she supplied space for fun and refreshments for a price. Margie had taken over Ma Sybil concession on the docks and she was doing well. Margie claimed American Indian descent through her mother's blood. With the claim of exotic plasma, she moved like a princess among the high brow of the sporting spree. Margie had stepped up a little higher in her impeccable ideology.

Margie first dive was geared for amusement for the common day work people. Now, she catered to the upper-class, undertakers, numbers king, railroad workers, salesmen, and clerk. The once bare floor and the cheap well worn linoleum had given way to rich red, plush, wall to wall carpet. The plain walls were kalmonized in various tones to match the furnishings. The windows were heavily, beautifully, and carefully draped. Golden corn liquor, the best that could ever be found in those parts of the country was served. Mellow Homebrewed which Margie made herself, soothed the palate of the customers. While young couples kept the air pervaded with soft melodious music, flowing from a roll piano.

With paper and pencil, Margie poised herself to write Rufus; just thinking about him as he walked down the stairs and waited for her at the bottom would make her laugh with joy. Rufus gave Margie such feelings of completeness, knowing that

CHAPTER FIFTEEN

whatever flights of fancy she took off in, he would be there when she came back. Waiting for her, unafraid, Margie had tears in her eyes and sadness in her heart. She did what she had to;

Dearest beloved Rufus:

You know that I would marry you immediately, if matters were different at home. Sometime ago, I revealed the story about my family to you. Since I am the first born, I feel that I have the duty to comfort my mother, should a crisis arise. I will never live in New York; that you may know by now. Maybe, someday I'll visit New York and too, I know that you will never live in Savannah. So with regret and great sorrow, I must release you. When you find a nice woman that you love and she loves you; with all my heart, you have my blessings. I do hope that your marriage will be a success. I, too, expect to marry some day and have children. Although, I haven't found the right man yet, I am still hoping.

Sincerely with love and regrets,

Margie Gamble
Margie Gamble

16

CHAPTER SIXTEEN

Gloria Staff and Dorothy Adams were roommates. A union dance was coming up and Gloria's boyfriend bought four tickets for the dance and gave them to his girlfriend to keep until the dance arrived. Gloria's boyfriend asked her to bring Dorothy to the dance; he had a man friend he wanted her to meet. Gloria asked Dorothy to come with them to the dance and she accepted. Gloria was so excited that Dorothy has accepted the invitation that she entrusted the tickets with Dorothy.

The night of the dance, the four started out forms the girls flat. They rode the train downtown. When they had reached the New York Hotel, where the dance was held, you could hear melodious music. The tingling of the piano, the beat of the drum, and the wailing of the saxophone were all heard harmonizing together.

"Tickets!" Gloria's arm extended with popping fingers and a foot that was tapping to the tempo of the tuneful music.

"Tickets!" Dorothy exclaimed. Then it flashed back to her. She had left the tickets tucked safely away in her bureau drawer. "Oh! Oh! I forgot them" Dorothy stated, blushing crimson, her brown eyes dilating and her bosom heaving. "I'll go back for them." Dorothy felt like a complete fool. How could she betray a trust like that?" she thought. "Just wait right here." Dorothy turned to go for the tickets. Gloria was speechless; her mouth agape as so was Dorothy's blind date.

"You'll do no such thing." Gloria's girlfriend placed a restraining hand on Dorothy's arm. "We'll just buy more tickets, that's all". Gloria's boyfriend fished into his pocket and came up with a bill.

"We've paid once." Dorothy's blind date rebelled, waving his arms into the air. "Now we'll buy tickets all over again."

"I'll pay!" Gloria boyfriend stated, handing the ticker taker a bill. "Don't worry about it. We're here to have a good time, not to argue about tickets."

"Don't play me cheap." Dorothy said, fumbling with her bag. Although, she knew that she didn't have that amount of money with her. "How could I be so stupid? I'm Sorry.' Dorothy berated herself.

"Forget it, kid". Gloria's boyfriend spoke. "It's all in the bag. Let's go in and shake."

The dance was very exciting; the well dressed guests twisted and turned on the glass like floor. After some drinks, Dorothy and the group were very elated and in a dancing mood. As they whirled to a fast moving tempo, Dorothy's date had a little too much of the potent firewater; one foot got tangled with the other and he fell prone to the floor. Dorothy whirled; her gestured was beautiful, indeed. She floated with the same candor as her pretty hair. Like magic, a pair of out stretched hands bated Dorothy. Without missing a beat, Dorothy waltzed into Rufus' arms.

Rufus' roving eyes had already admired Dorothy's graceful moments on the dance floor. He liked the stunning green grown she wore. That's how Rufus and Dorothy met. "Fate! Fate!" Rufus said. They often laugh about that night.

"Any man who couldn't stand on his feet, hold his liquor and a pretty girl, deserved to be danced over." Rufus laughed. The fallen man, after a few attempts to rise as the floor was slippery, finally scrambled to his feet. Dorothy's blind date was furious; he stood on the side and waited until the tune was finished, the ticket was fuel enough, now Dorothy had added more fuel.

"I want to talk to you!" The fallen one said, grabbing the arm of Dorothy greedily. "You don't have any respect for you escort, do you? At least you should have waited until I was on my feet before you grabbed your man. Why didn't you tell me that you had someone waiting for you to dance?"

"I don't know that man." Dorothy said. "I never saw him before." Dorothy was rescued by Gloria's boyfriend.

"Look man, tonight is not your night." Gloria's date spoke. "We must be extra careful going back. The fucking train might blow up, with you on it." That drew a smile from all and the fun was resumed. There were other dances and Rufus and Dorothy exchanged addresses and a romantic blossomed. One year later, they got married.

The morning after Rufus and Dorothy's wedding, they remained in bed late. The Niagara Falls sunshine from a crack in the shutter, permitting the light to creep across them. They kissed, talked, made love, and listened to the chatter of the birds.

"I love you very much, Rufus." Dorothy confessed, snuggling up to Rufus as tears of joy flowed from her eyes. "I'm happier now, at this moment that I've been in my whole life."

CHAPTER SIXTEEN

"I'm happy too." Rufus stated, embracing Dorothy tight. "I'm certainly glad that I was at that dance."

After they returned to New York, one morning, Dorothy glanced from their window. Her eyes picked up the weathered flag that was mounted on the post office. The torn material flapped on its pole, and the flags semblance was an eagle winging about and unable to fly away.

Dorothy remembered the first nightmare that Rufus had after they were married. Rufus finally imparted his secret to Dorothy. In nightmare, Ma Sybil died and Rufus and his sister were separated, he was trying to find them. He climbed a tall fence and on the way down his shirt tail got caught on the fence. His screaming was so loud, Dorothy awoke him. That was the constant demon that haunted Rufus. Dorothy sympathized with Rufus, because her parents were still alive and together.

The storm has wondered out to sea. Rufus thought for a brief moment he was living in Yamacraw, a restless simple lad. He was choked up and didn't want to think further. Reminiscing about circumstances in the past still haunted him. What's wrong with me, he thought. "I'm married to a good woman, who teaches high-school. I have a good job at the docks. My sisters are married. All but Rena Mae. I don't think Rena Mae wants to be married, she likes the life that she is living.

When Rufus remembered Yamacraw, he thought of the June bugs. In July, the children of Yamacraw were too poor to afford kites, and most didn't know how to build one. They caught June bugs and tied a cord on one leg and held onto the cord and watched the June bugs sail like a kite humming as they went. Nature's kite on a string.

Although Dorothy's parents didn't shower affection on her, she knew they loved her. And whenever she needed them they were there. Dorothy's father, Fred Adams, and her mother, Nina, worked next door to each other. Fred was a cab driver and Nina worked at a boutique.

Two months after Dorothy was born, Nina left her with her blind sister, Emma. Emma was disabled by an explosion at a chemical plant where she worked in New Jersey. Emma attended a school for the blind; she learned to read and write Braille and to care for herself. Aunt Emma took Dorothy with her everywhere she went. She bought Dorothy her first second-hand piano, paid for her music lessons and her first hay-hay ride. She also paid for her first year college tuition.

Aunt Emma was able to live a pleasant and happy life from the accident funds. She devoted most of her time to her niece. Nina, Dorothy's mother, said that Emma was spoiling the child. Emma paid her sister no heed, she lavished tenderness and material effects on Dorothy.

"My word!" Nina said to her husband. "Should Emma die before I do, she'll probably leave me a hundred dollars at most, everything will go to Dorothy."

"Wait a minute," Fred spoke, frowning a bit as he stared at his wife. "Let's not be greedy. What if Emma leaves everything to Dorothy? It's still in the family, isn't it? Nina angrily mumbled nebulous words and ambled to the bathroom.

Nina was distraught about her sister losing her sight. But she was glad that Emma hadn't stopped living. Dorothy displayed more affection for her Aunt Emma that she did her mother.

Aunt Emma was so understanding and thoughtful. At times, when Dorothy was around her she felt transparent. Dorothy perceived as though, Aunt Emma was seeing right through her, reading her mind and feeling the pain in her body. To Dorothy that was a mystical feeling.

After Dorothy and Rufus son was born, she would get lonesome for her family; especially Aunt Emma. On weekends, Dorothy bundled her family together and took off to Stamford, Connecticut. She didn't have Aunt Emma to nurture her son, Rufus Hannibal, V. She placed her son in the nursery, which was in her building. The nursery was owned and operated by Craig's mother.

CHAPTER SIXTEEN

Craig was Rufus' best friend. They were all from Savannah, Georgia. Dorothy and Rufus knew it was safe to leave their son with Craig's mother.

Rena Mae, window-shopping on 125th Street, gave a peripheral glance. Sizing her up, was a tall handsome man. He approached her. "See anything that you like? I'll buy it for you. My name is Brain Allen. What's yours?' Brain smiled and Rena Mae grinned that silly grin that she was known to do.

"My name is Rena Mae Hannibal." "That's a nice pair of shoes there." Brian pointed to the shoes. "Would you like them?" Rena Mae grinned. "Do you mean that?"

"Of course, I mean it." Brian said. "Let's go inside and see if they have your size." The shoes were a perfect fit. After the shopping, they sauntered to Brian's three-room flat.

Brain persuaded Rena Mae to move in with him. It was a lovely romance, both tall, banana colored, good looking and well dressed. Their erotic affair lasted about a year. Up until that time Rena Mae had never held a regular job. Her usual way, was, to shack-up with a man, at her place or his. When something went wrong, Rena Mae would make a quick exit. She was ambitious, loved money and all the nice things that it could buy, but she didn't like to work for them. Although Rena Mae had all the essentials at home, she became restless and began to cheat on Brian. His friend informed him about Rena Mae's other lover.

Brian's mother died when he was fifteen years old. His two sisters brought him to New York, from Charlotte, North Carolina, to live with them. He shared the four-room apartment with his single sisters. The sisters worked in the Garment Center, and soon Brian was hired as a floor-boy. Brian learned to repair sewing machines and soon he was head mechanic. He prided himself on his task and when he was nineteen, he rented a flat.

Brain needed just one year to finish high school, but he never went back. After work, Brian and his comrades, who are less educated than he, passed their time, standing on the street corners, clowning. They hopped bars on 120th Street and dated the chicks. Brian and his friends spent most of their salaries on expensive clothes and Florheim shoes. Brian's special cut clothes had style and they did him credit. He would brag about his costly outfits and accessories, and that he had the same tailor as Duke Ellington.

As the women passed the streets, "Who is that chick?" Inquired one of Brian's cronies as an unknown woman strolled by. "I'll like to have some of that." Spoke another. "Look at the babe in the yellow dress. I'll like to have some of that hump." Said another guy. "I bet that booty is real good, man." "Of, course, that one I can speak from experience."

The group chuckled for the statement. "Man you can't handle that." The speaker continued. "You too light, man! You need a saddle to stay on her. Man, that gal will throw you out of bed." The whole group chuckles. Brain and friends were living in the world that they enjoyed. It gave them a little cocky pleasure to brag about their conquests. It never occurred to them to buy a house, someplace on the island. And at that time, houses were very reasonable in Queens and other parts of Long Islands.

The lovely spring trees were vividly green. Children lightly clad, skipped and hopped on the pavement. Lightly opened coats revealed the smooth bare throats of the people that were a token as charming as the first Forsythia plants.

In spite of Rena Mae's infidelity, Brian's flat was well kept. His clothes in order and his meals were waiting, ready when he came home. Brain was upset about the news concerning Rena Mae being unfaithful to him. He wanted to detect Rena Mae in the act. One day he took off from work without Rena Mae knowing. Brian did that a few times without any luck, and became very angry. He began to complain about this shirts, they didn't have enough starch. The house wasn't clean and the food wasn't properly cooked. This was a lie, Rena Mae was an excellent cook and housekeeper.

Brian couldn't hold the news about Rena Mae any longer. He finally approached her with what he had heard. Rena Mae denied the rumor, but a fight ensured anyway. Rena Mae ended up with a black eye and swollen face. Of Course, she fought

fought back and Brain's face showed the proof. Brain had done the ungodly act that Rena Mae would not accept, disfiguring her face. They didn't go out that weekend. Brain was sorry for the attack and he tried to patch things up by providing Rena Mae with additional funds. Brain went to work feeling good, he had everything out in the open.

Around ten o'clock that morning Rena Mae left the flat and traveled all the way uptown. She found a room near 8th avenue and 15th street. Rena Mae packed her belongings and moved out. She abhorred any man who attacked her physically.

When Brain got home Rena Mae wasn't there. Brain looked about the place and he knew that Rena Mae had left. Brian strode to her bar, bought drinks and made inquires about Rena Mae. No one had seen her that day. Brain put fliers out to find Rena Mae, then he got drunk and staggered home.

For the first time in her life Rena Mae decided to get a job. After combing downtown, Rena Mae was finally hired as a chambermaid, at a fashionable hotel. Almost, instantly an alliance sprung up between Rena Mae and the head bellhop. Strangely enough, Rena Mae liked the job, the tips, and the many flirtations with the men about the hotel. She explained to her new lover that she could only receive guests in drawing room. This wasn't a major problem, because Rena Mae had a friend, who had a flat and they spent much time there.

It took sometime before Brain found Rena Mae, although he had ears out for her. Finally, Brain's friend informed him where Rena Mae lived. When Rena Mae heard that Brian knew her whereabouts, she armed herself with what she called a Georgia ten cents pistol. The ten cents pistol consisted of a mixture of piss and red devil lye. Rena Mae carried the pint mayonnaise jar capped very tightly, with her everywhere she went. One Friday night, she and her lover been visiting a friend, and they left after midnight.

Brain had been waiting for Rena Mae a long time. While waiting and drinking, he became very hungry. The composite smell of food cooking assaulted his nostrils and he entered a restaurant. Although Brain wasn't religious, he ordered a red snapper dinner and a bottle of white wine. The wine came first and as he sipped the wine, his mind's eye was on Rena Mae. The wine suited Brain right down to his very toenails. After he had finished his dinner, he went bar hopping until midnight. When the wine was consumed, Brain bought a bottle of Old Crow. He quaffed from the bottle and it brought all the ugliness that was in him.

Brain was puffing heavily as he crouched behind some high steps. He glanced at his watch, and became very agitated. Then suddenly, time stopped for Brain as he emerged from his concealed place. Rena Mae stepping lively wore a black Cashmere coat with a thick, white mink collar. She had never been so ravishing to Brain.

As Rena Mae emerged from subway, the night was frosty and icy. Rena Mae looked up at the sky. It was beautiful, clear, and the stars pierced through the midnight sky. Rena Mae sucked in the chilled air, her honeydew breast reared as she tossed her head. She was like a vixen, something crazily exciting. Her eyelids had been dampened with a thin metallic, light blue paint. Rena Mae's eyelashes were absurdly thick and seemed to weight her eyelids down as if with shame. Rena Mae's good, firm steps were almost athletic. She took unusual long graceful strides, as her companion sauntered by her side. At that moment, Rena Mae eyes picked up Brian.

"There he is. Trouble is brewing". Rena Mae insisted. "You just cross the street as though you don't know me." The lover consented.

Rena Mae was as a young, wild, mustang, suddenly invaded by a young lion. She saw that Brain was drunk and she knew that her foul mouth could no longer shield her from that hardened animal. The one courteous, loving, hospitable, meek person now became mean and ugly. A friend had alerted Rena Mae, that Brain had said that if he couldn't have her no one was going to have her. When he finished wither the buzzard wouldn't want her.

CHAPTER SIXTEEN

Rena Mae quickly but steadily opened her purse. She had rehearsed the affair over and over in her mind, for weeks. She unscrewed the lid off the jar but kept it in her bag and her hand on the jar. Rena Mae continued to walk forward holding onto the mayonnaise jar. As Brain neared Rena Mae, he raised his arm with the long shiny knife in his hand. Rena Mae saw her life fade away. Almost simultaneously when the knife struck Rena Mae's neck, she stepped backwards, screamed. And with one swift dash, the acid for the jar splashed Brain's face. The impact from the bottle was so powerful that Brain fell to the pavement. The sound was so great, it sound like a five hundred pounds of bailed cotton dropping form a wagon.

"Rena Mae, please! Please!" Brain wailed, still striking his head against the sidewalk. The alarm went off, the bell was silent for a while then Brain worked assiduously toward consciousness. The black Cashmere coat with a thick, white mink collar, kept Rena Mae's neck for being detached from her body. The knife made a small imprint on Rena Mae's flesh, just enough to draw a trickle of blood. Rena Mae glanced down at Brain lying at her feet with the weapon still clutched in his hand. The smooth street came spinning and sailing up at Rena Mae, but the heavy crash of Brain's body against the sidewalk brought Rena Mae back to reality. Done for, she thought. Rena Mae's body became weak, she ran screaming, toward the corner clutching her handbag.

Rena Mae's strength ebbing, and her feet like a block of iron as she ran. Rena Mae groaned and almost fell to the ground. She imagined that the knife was in her back. She ran with outstretched flapping arms, like an eagle preparing for a flight. Then, help me! Somebody help me! A woman went to Rena Mae. "What's the matter dear?" Rena Mae told the woman that she wanted to call her brother. The woman pointed out a telephone to her. "I'm so nervous, I can't dial. Will you dial the number for me?" Rena Mae asked.

"Of course, I will." The good lady replied. Rufus answered the phone and through the hysterics, Rena Mae told

Rufus what had happen. Rufus asked where she was. Rena Mae explained to him the location. Rufus told her to stay in the phone booth until he got there. "Don't let anyone in the booth. Don't let anybody in,' Rufus instructed. Rufus called his lawyer and asked him to meet him at the designated street and phone booth.

"Who is it?" Dorothy asked as Rufus hurried to put on his clothes. Rufus's leg missed the pant leg, backed all the way across the room, and landed against the dresser with such a clatter that some of Dorothy's toiletries fell to the floor.

"That was Rena Mae." Rufus answered. "She is in big trouble and I must get to her right away."

"Shall I come with you?" Dorothy questioned, now sitting up in the bed. "No, I'll see you later." Rufus replied. "I'll take care of it." As he kissed Dorothy and rushed out the room.

When Rufus arrived at the scene a large crowd had gathered, the police cars lights were flashing and an ambulance was approaching with sirens full blast. Rufus went to the phone booth where Rena Mae was held up. Rufus knocked on the door

to face Rena Mae physiognomy drenched with tears. Simultaneously, Rufus' lawyer stepped from a cab. He and Rufus
conferred to what had happened. The three walked over to where
Brain was lying on the street, with the knife still clutched in his
hand.

The police retrieved the knife from Brain's hand. "The
Zigger Boos are raising hell tonight," one cop expressed. "Friday
night, you, know. Pay day." Another laughed. "She sure fixed
him. He got all juiced up, lying wait to harm her. Well, she
showed him a thing or two. I don't think he will do that again."
The third policeman stated.

"No, that's if he ever sees again." The forth officer cack-
led. "The stench of alcohol coming from him is enough to knock
you out." A cop said, walking to the ambulance as they loaded
Brain in. still floating in Rena Mae's memory when she was a
child. Ma Sybil took her shopping and it was the first time she
had seen a person's face with discoloration. Rena Mae asked her
granny what was wrong with the person's face. Ma Sybil ex-

plained to her about acid, when it had contact with skin. When Rena Mae was growing up, she discussed the acid matter with some friends. Friends told her in order to make the substance stronger, mix it with piss and that was better that a gun. So that was why they called it the Savannah ten cents pistol. A can cost ten cents.

Brain's sisters lover their only brother and they would do anything to help him. The sisters were never married and they had no children. The sister engaged a very competent derma-tologist to correct the disfigured condition on Brian's face.

When Brain was well enough to appear in court the judge asked, "Rena Mae, what you want to be done to Brain?" Your honor, all I ask is that Brain never bother me again." Rena Mae expressed hardly.

"Brain, do you have in mind to bother Rena Mae again?" The judge questioned, as he stared into Brain's eyes. "No sir, I will never bother that woman again," he said. "That is fine." The judge spoke. "Make sure that you keep your word." "Yes, sir,

I'll keep my word." Brian assured the judge, "I'll never get that drunk again." "Make sure, that you don't." The judge continued, "Case closed."

Despite the general tumult, threats, and the effectual patching of shattered things. Rena Mae had perception enough to realize that she lived through the end of an era. Rena Mae thought about the advice Ma Sybil had given her: 'Take care of your baby, you might need her someday'. Rena Mae knew that she wanted her child; in fact she needed her, even though she knew that she had little communication with her daughter since she was born.

Occasionally, Rena Mae would send Kay a photo of herself, a dress and a pair of shoes, but that was all the connection she had with Kay since she had been with the Starks. Rena Mae was now approaching forty. She was still attractive, but her calculation, shamelessness, exaltation, vileness of mouth and her diabolic manner exceeded all belief.

CHAPTER SIXTEEN

Rena Mae thought about the surging desire in her body as a young girl; her curious, pure nectarine beginning, without pain, down-home in Yamacraw. The hormones working through her being, gave her the wonderful, strange, sweet taste of love with Jim Nelson. A feeling that she had long ago known when Kay was conceived. Rena Mae decided that she must get Kay; she would go on welfare. Kay would receive a good education. Rena Mae's health hadn't been good lately. Her features were slowly fading and she had trouble with her men; but the Brain episode, that was the last straw. What Rena Mae wanted now was basic shelter and food. The rest she would scrap up some-how.

Rena Mae's cousin, who still lived in Savannah, kept in touch. At intervals, she kept Rena Mae posted concerning the Starks and her daughter. For years, the Starks went to Cape May, New Jersey during the summer to pick beans and other vegeta-bles. So after the Brian episode, Rena Mae wrote her cousin to find out where the Starks were going to be the next picking time.

Rena Mae made her move. After planning, she took the bus to Cape May, then hired a taxi to take her to the field. When Rena Mae arrived at the number of the cottage, she asked the driver to wait; she was going for her daughter. When she entered the cottage, Kay was making dinner. Mrs. Stark was lying on a cot in the front room. Mr. Stark was still in the field. Rena Mae walked into the small kitchen and grabbed Kay by the arm. "Come on! I'm taking you out of here right now," Rena Mae puffed. "I'm going to put you in a good school so you can get a first rate education." Rena Mae said, tugging at Kay's arm.

"Mama! Mama!" Kay still tried to reach the only mother she knew. "Mama come and help me." Kay was bracing her foot against the door and holding onto the doorknob. Mrs. Starks heard the commotion and sat up on the cot.

"It's you Rena Mae." Mrs. Stark spoke, getting up from the cot. "No, Rena Mae. You can't take her like that. You must wait until her father comes home."

CHAPTER SIXTEEN

"Oh, yes I can." Rena Mae yelled. "What do you mean, her father? That old black, ugly man isn't my child's father. Kay's father is in Newark, New Jersey. Jim Nelson wants to see his oldest child." Although Jim had married and had a family, Rena Mae and Jim had managed to keep in touch through the years.

"Mama! Mama!" Kay still calling and trying to reach Mrs. Stark. "That old woman isn't your mother." Rena Mae voiced angrily. "I'm your mother and stop pulling against me. Stop calling that woman Mama, I mean it." Suddenly, Rena Mae's hand flew out and struck Kay about the face and it produced a yelp of dismay. "Don't you recognize me from the photo I sent you?" Rena Mae walked out dragging the bare-footed Kay, mumbling. "The nerve of that woman, lying in bed and got my child cooking for her. Well, Kay won't cook anymore dinners for her."

Mrs. Stark stood in the door, her face a river. "No, Rena Mae. Wait until her father comes home!" Mrs. Stark pleaded. "Bring Kay back; please don't take her that way".

Rena Mae gave Mrs. Stark no heed. She didn't even thank her for keeping her child for more than thirteen years. Once in the cab, Rena Mae yanked the faded dress off and flung it to the floor of the cab. She pulled a new dress over Kay's head and put a new pair of sneakers on, which were too tight. Rena Mae dressed Kay while the cab was still moving to the bus stop and from there to New York City.

Mrs. Stark slowly walked to the field to inform her husband about what had happened. When Mr. Stark saw his wife with tearful eyes, he swiftly walked to her and asked, "What's the matter, dear?"

"Rena Mae took Kay." Mrs. Stark cried as she wiped the tears from her eyes. "Rena Mae wouldn't wait until you came from the fields. I pleaded with her to wait, but she wouldn't." "Don't worry dear". Mr. Stark spoke as he wiped tears from his eyes. "As nice as we were to her and her child... Rena Mae has no heart. She won't have good luck. Rena Mae is heartless".

"What will we do without our baby?" Mrs. Stark lamented. "We'll survive." Mr. Stark answered, still wiping away the tears. "We still have our two sons and their children." They strolled back to the cabin, arm in arm, not believing what had just happened and how it happened.

Rena Mae forbade Kay from communicating with the Starks in any way. And if she did, she would know. Besides, it's too dangerous. She could be charged with kidnapping. If she was locked up, they would place her in a foster home. So, Kay complied with Rena Mae's wishes. Kay never forgave Rena Mae for what she did and how she did it. Kay never had close feelings for Rena Mae. She didn't resent Rena Mae because she abandoned her as a baby. She couldn't have been left in a better home. So, Kay silently hankered for the mother she had known all of her life.

Immediately, Rena Mae contacted the social services with Kay. She told them that her grandmother had died and she kept Kay. Rena Mae had the birth certificate from Savannah, Georgia, so she got help.

Rena Mae took Kay to see Rufus, Lulu, and the family. She gleefully told them how she took her child form the old folks. "They were making her a slave out of my child. Kay was cooking their meal and the woman was sleeping on a cot". Rena Mae said.

"Well, since you took her in such a rude manner," Rufus stated, "at least you should write them a letter and apologize." "Apologize! Apologize for what?" Rena Mae shouted. "I saved my child's life, and besides, they will have me locked up for kidnapping." "No they won't." Lulu expressed, feeling some of the pain that the Starks were now feeling. "Rena Mae, you should have more sympathy for other people. You have created a situation that needs to be corrected."

"Whether they would do anything or not," Rena Mae shouted, "I'm not writing them and Kay dare not contact them, either."

Rufus', Zenna's, and Lulu's attitudes were different from Rena Mae's. Their well-ordered lives from meager existence flowed on peacefully, untroubled by mud, fleas, cockroaches, and the many insects that covered the universe.

Kay finished high school and married soon after, to a classmate. Kay's husband was a relief. He worked as a railroad clerk for the Rapid Transit. He later trained for a motorman. Kay worked as a nurse's aid, while studying to become a Registered Nurse. She told her husband about how Rena Mae had deserted her as a baby and how she snatched her away from the only family she knew. Kay's husband was appalled about the situation. Kay and her husband vowed to never allow Rena Mae to live with them. She would be welcomed to spend the night or a few weeks, but never live there, never.

Since Rena Mae lived in New York, she had about thirty addresses and probably more in Savannah. Rena Mae never rented a flat and flats were reasonable when she arrived in New York, she rented rooms with cooking privileges and she never had a telephone. Rena Mae's stability was like the character Edgar Allen Poe's novel and her morals were the same. Kay told her husband that since she had been on New York, she was hurting inside, but thee wasn't anyone to talk to about the situation. Kay's husband instructed her to sit down and write the Stark's family. He told her to ask them to forgive her and explain the whole episode to them concerning Rena Mae. He advised her to send their wedding photos and ten dollars.

One year after Kay's marriage, a healthy son was born. They named him Dan, after Kay's foster father. They sent a photo of baby Dan and told them when they were financially able they would visit them. All this was happening without Rena Mae's knowledge. One year later, Kay gave birth to a healthy girl and they named her Lizzie, after her foster mother. The

CHAPTER SIXTEEN

Starks were the most loving and beautiful people in the whole world to Kay. Kay's foster brothers were kind to her as well as helped her with her homework and gave her piggyback rides. Kay didn't hate her birth mother, but she wasn't close to her either. Rena Mae sensed it.

17

CHAPTER SEVENTEEN

Zenna and Sam had twenty years of complete bliss, until one day as Sam was driving along the streets and braked for a light; their lives changed. A study flow of raindrops splashed the city, four female teenagers with books, playfully and gleefully trying to shelter themselves under one umbrella shrieked, "Taxi." Sam smiled and looked over. My word, Zenna, Sam thought. One of the girls had long braids wrapped around her youthful head and a pretty face stared at Sam. Sam's mind swung back more than twenty years when he first saw Zenna. He leaned over and opened the door. "May I drop you girls some-place?" Sam was eyeing the girl with the long braids, as she smiled faintly. "It's going to be very hard for four pretty girls to shelter under one umbrella." Sam spoke, still holding the door open. The girls piled into the back seat, but soon they began to complain about the crowded conditions.

"You're sitting on my books." One of the girls objected. "Get off my lap." Another protested. Sam glanced into the rear-view mirror at them.

"Hey, you with the long braids," Sam stated with a slight trace of a smile flittering across his face, "You may come up front with me, that's if you're not afraid". "Who me?" The fresh girl crawled over the seat, her short plaid skirt surged up, displaying her tempting golden smooth flesh. Sam's penis stood at attention.

"My name is Sam Dorkins." He gave her another glance. "What's your?" "My name is Beatrice." She said coquette. "Beatrice Felt". She looked at Sam in a way she had never looked at a man before, as though she was assessing Sam's ability as a man.

"Pretty name and a very pretty girl." Sam winked at her. "Where do I drop you girls?" Sam asked as he sailed down the street. "Straight ahead," Beatrice smiled and ran her hand tantalizing down her thigh and tugged at her skirt, "five blocks more, we can walk the rest of the way."

"I would like to see you sometime, Beatrice." Sam said as he eyed her. "If that's possible?"

"Yes, you may pick me up any evening after school". Beatrice snickered, touching her glossy hair and gold earring. A joyous kind of restlessness swept over her. It seemed like all the distilled jollity in the world had taken residence in her young body. "And in this shiny, sharp car." Beatrice spoke as she banged the door shut. Sam chuckled and sped off, while the girls giggled, pushed and pecked at one another.

"Well, wasn't that a come on, if I ever saw one", Sam thought. "Beatrice did everything to temp me, a very fresh kid, not that I mind and she is pretty too. No Sam Dorkins, that's not for you, you are a very happily married man. Well, I just want to see if I still had it. Yes I do. Sam old boy, you still floor them. Heah! Lay down boy", Sam said tapping his penis lightly as he braked the car in front of his house.

It wasn't known whether Sam was unfaithful to Zenna before Beatrice came into his life. He tried to put Beatrice out of his mind, but she just wouldn't go. After school, Beatrice waited for Sam at a designated spot, and they went places. Beatrice stirred something in Sam and he was restless. Sam was in a continual quagmire of excitement. He had many restful years with Zenna, no man could have had a better wife; they were very compatible.

Zenna was unfortunate with her pregnancies and after some miscarriages, her doctor warned her not to try again, it was too dangerous. Sam and Zenna were prosperous and they shared the same business enterprise. Sam and Zenna were active in the community programs. Zenna considered herself the epitome of an intelligent, polished, established, black woman; well put together.

Zenna enlarged the four-room house to seven rooms. She remodeled and landscaped the entire placed. Zenna was very ambitious; flowers and fruit trees adorned the area. Zenna's hands were never still. She studied "notary public" and income tax filing.

When Zenna wasn't busy with clients in the store, she knitted sweaters, scarves, and socks. Those items she displayed in the shop's windows. The money from the sale of the articles went into a separate bank account under the name of Kay Hannibal, Zenna's niece, Rena Mae's daughter.

Zenna explained to Sam why she wanted to put the money into a separate account. Kay had a hard life. Zenna told Sam that when Kay was a month old, Rena Mae gave her away as though she was a cat or dog, just so she could live a wild life. Kay deserved better than that. Sam agreed with Zenna and said that the money would definitely go to Kay.

For six months, Sam had a gleam in his eyes for Beatrice, a beam like a soap bubble, shining in the sunlight. Sam existed under that spell and became distant to Zenna. After sleeping with Beatrice part of the night, he took her home and returned to the hotel for the rest of the night. Sam never stayed out all night before without an explanation. He was obsessed with Beatrice. He had carefully retraced his steps with her from the first day he saw her. Sam recalled the first time he declared his love for Beatrice and she declared her love for him. His body exploded into flame every time he thought about her.

One day during lunch, Sam and Zenna sat at the table eating. Sam, while picking at the pieces of red tomatoes, oranges, carrots and green cucumbers that were in his salad, Sam spoke. "Zenna, I have a confession to make." He finally made up his mind to tell Zenna everything.

"Zenna, I'm in love. Really in love." Sam reported. "Once I felt this way about you, but since we've been together so long, I hardly get it up for you. Sometimes, I can't, you know that. I've met a seventeen year old girl, Beatrice. And now, I'm hard all the time for her. Zenna, I want a divorce, so that I can marry Beatrice."

Although the words were articulated, but they ricocheted off Zenna's brain like a volley of missiles. When Zenna was calmer, she said, "What kind of nonsense is this?" Hoping that Sam was teasing her as he sometimes did. Zenna had heard that Sam was seeing a young girl, but she didn't think much about it. She also knew that Sam was staying out late and without explanation, even when she asked for one. So she ignored the whole episode.

"It isn't nonsense, Zenna." Sam stated, looking deep into Zenna's eyes. "I hope you appreciate my honesty. You know our policy, to be honest with each other; until a few months ago, I wasn't very honest."

"Of course we have, at least I have." Zenna raised her arm as though to ward of a blow. "Sam, to run around with a seventeen year old girl is one thing, but to ask me to free you so that you can marry that pip squeak, that's more than I expect of you. I gave you more credit for having more intelligence than that.' Zenna frowned on the subject like a giant fortress pursued against an invasion. "Sam, please don't insult my intelligence."

"Zenna, I'm not joking." Same spoke. "I really mean it. I want a divorce. Zenna I can't get it up for you sometimes, you know that. With Beatrice, I'm up and ready in an instant."

"Sam, I know that sometimes you can't get it up, but that's not what marriage is all about." Zenna spoke harshly. "Marriage is when two people grow old together, and one gets sick, one of them will be there to wipe the shit off their asses. Now tell me, where will Beatrice be when you get sick and you need her?"

"Beatrice will be there. I just know it." Sam said quickly. "And besides, where will she find a man as rich as me?"

"Sam, you've met this pissy tail bitch and you think that I'll walk out of your life, just like that?" Zenna snapped her fingers. "Now, if you want to make a fool of yourself over a young girl, that's your business. You are not going to marry her. I'm not leaving this house. I've heard about the slut and her mother. Her mother has a dressmaking establishment and if this keeps up, I will confront her concerning the matter. I'll make such a stink, the scandal won't help her mother's business."

The sentence was like a pastoral poem to Sam's aural. "I can't be made unhappy because of you woman. I must be free. You place me in a painful position. I must be free and I will be free. Zenna, you're despicable!" Sam charged.

"Despicable or not, Sam, you are not getting a divorce." Zenna expressed angrily.

"Zenna, I will get a divorce from you." Sam face growing painful. He arose from his chair and sauntered over to Zenna frowning. Suddenly, a terrible blow on Zenna head that tore her feet from under her and she landed toward the door. Zenna's head struck the floor jam and she whimpered like a struck puppy. Sam strode to the fridge and took out a can of beer. Zenna laid there for a moment, but fear and pride lifted her. She jumped up with fright and vigor. She quickly picked up an old flat iron that was used for a doorstop. With all her strength, Zenna aimed the iron at Sam's back as he stood drinking the beer. The iron landed on target. The beer spewed from Sam's mouth and the can fell to the floor. Sam shook his head disapprovingly and doubled over. When he straightened up and looked around, Zenna was gone. Sam hobbled to the door, but he was in such pain that the didn't give a chase.

The summer was dry, the lightening tore the sky into jiggered liquid fragments. An ominous peal of thunder was heard everywhere and the torrential rain refreshed the earth. Zenna mooning her life away as she trudged about her tasks. She lifted her head in the hope that she would catch the sound of Sam's footsteps. Perhaps, he would exchange a word with her, a smile. Zenna hoped for a word, a crumb, a nod of the head, something that would keep her going another day. But what she got was the silent treatment or an outburst for total freedom from her.

Zenna looked at Sam and in the depth of her soul she wanted him to be punished for his infidelity. Zenna wanted Sam to suffer for ruining her peace of mind and her honor.

Zenna refused to walk out of Sam's life. Zenna's deterrence gave her complete satisfaction and a measure of comfort. Sam's sowing wild oats would pass. Yes, time heals all things and someday we'll be compatible again, Zenna thought. After all, Sam's seventeen years older than me, what would he do with a young girl? Some nights, Zenna would lie in bed and listen for Sam footsteps. When the house began to vibrate as Sam strode in, without knowing why Zenna smiled; recollecting that she was waiting for him. Zenna love Sam deep down into the recesses of her heart.

For a while, Zenna was a person bereft of reason. She stared motionless and unconsciously. She was completely covered with ignominy, and was overcome and confused. Zenna was startled, irritated, and full of tears, misery, despair and breathless shame. Everything she had jealously guarded and concealed had now been laid bare. However, in Zenna's agony and enforced anguish, the situation left a serious impression on her. Zenna displayed two black eyes very ostentatiously. When Aunt Julia confronted her, Zenna gave some sort of fictitious happenings. Of course, Aunt Julia had heard about Sam and Beatrice, and the fight that was going on between Sam and Zenna.

Aunt Julia went straight to the subject of abuse that Zenna had received from Sam. "Zenna, if you and Sam are not getting alone very well," Aunt Julia spoke sadly, "maybe it's best for you to leave him."

"Everything is fine, Aunt Julia." Zenna assured, shrugging her shoulders. "You know how a man can be sometimes. It's nothing to be alarmed about." Zenna remembered her first husband, Timmy; and how the whole family had suffered because of it. She wasn't about to complain and get her family involved in her affairs, no matter what. She was going to swallow her pride and take it like a woman.

When Sam did come home late at night, he turned his back to his wife and snored soundly. Sam soon moved out of their bedroom. The old itch soon seized Sam. One night, he marched into Zenna's room and surveyed it with experienced eyes. He held a whiskey bottle, then guzzled from it. He staggered, swayed and knocked down from the mantel an urn of fresh flowers. The urn broke, Zenna stoutly maintained silent as she heard another crash. Sam smashed the empty whiskey bottle against the brick hearth, Russian style. He was like a hog, good for neither milk nor wool, Zenna thought.

Zenna paid no heed to Sam's demand to free him. Her servility was like that if a clumsy dog, always anticipating a blow from its master; even was welcoming it. She wanted her marriage to last to death.

Zenna was a missionary of good; she was goodness itself; the very embodiment of Christian spirit that forgave everything and everybody. Zenna devoted much of her time to other people, helping them and worrying about their troubles.

She was always thoughtful of others first and was appalled by Rena Mae. The prime fool of the family she thought. She loved Rena Mae and she never told her how to live her life.

Sam was drinking heavily; he swam in the tide of ale and other spirits. Zenna was perishing like a peach tree eaten form the roots by a borer. "I'll tell you this," Sam made a little elliptical gesture with his hand that held his glass with liquor; "you better let me go Zenna. We just can't make anymore, baby everything between us is dead. Dead! Dead as hell, I tell you."

"Sam, if you let that slut, 'cheerio-oat' make a fool out of you, that's too bad". Zenna strode from the stove with her eyes cast down and a sort of melancholy, but dignity pervaded her figure. She placed the breakfast on the table. "Sam, everything between us isn't dead, and you know it'. Zenna smiled as if it was a jest. "Sam, you're going through an erratic state, men do at your age. It's nothing to be ashamed about. I've seen Beatrice; she is young and pretty. I know that my youth is gone and so is yours. I'm not repulsive, neither are you. We've aged very well,

Sam. You're still a ladies' man. Maybe, you can hold your own with Beatrice, but for how long? Come now, Sam; let's be sensible. Remember that you're seventeen years older than me."

"Yes, I know." Sam bellowed. "Now let me tell you where do you come in, bitch?"

Zenna blared her eyes. "Remember the whole place has been renovated. Now the house has seven rooms, and the store has been enlarged. We have a beautiful garden, front and back yard and I landscaped everything. And certainly, I've worked and helped to accumulate the money that we have in the joint account."

"Bitch, you must be crazy!" Sam spoke with hostility and deliberated roughness. "You're not getting anything, not a damn thing. All you get is your clothes. That's all you came with and that's all you're going with. Everything here is mine; mine; mine. All mine!"

"I'll see about that, Sam." Zenna threw her head back and said quietly. "I've been patient with you Sam, I'm willing to wait until this capricious act is passed. But if you insist with this foolishness, I'll see an attorney and tie-up everything. I'm not joking, Sam. I'm on the trot form sunrise until late at night. I've given all my youthful years and I'm still giving. I can't work, just for food and clothes. I'm not a slave, Sam. I'm your wife. I'll tie-up everything, I mean it!"

Zenna means it, Sam thought. He marched over to Zenna, eyeing her frantically. His skin clouded, his nose quivered and the veins stood out on his temples. He acted as though he disapproved of his wife's cavalier perception, on such a grave matter. "Now, that's a fool idea!" Sam said, puckering-up his lips and rolling his eyes viciously.

"You can't stop me from marrying Beatrice!" Sam raised his hand to the morning stubbles on his chin.

"Oh, but I can stop you." Zenna smiled with a joyous agitation. She buttered her bread methodically, the way she did most of the time, when she felt irritated. She then settled herself into her chair to study the contents of his words.

"And how do you intend to do that?" Sam swallowed the last drops of his liquor in the glass and then he banged it down hard on the table; the glass broke. Zenna flinched at the unexpected backfire, disturbing her trend of thoughts. After a brief pause, she continued, "I've just told you, I'll tie-up everything." Zenna continued to chew her food. "Sam, you either had a bad night or your conscience is bothering you." Zenna spoke sourly and grimaced. "I'm not in the mood for an argument this morning."

"An argument! Who the hell is asking for an argument? I'm demanding my freedom or I'll kill you, bitch." Sam's hand went splash across Zenna's face. Her senses reeled and the smile slipped from her face. Sam was a brutal machine, with the advantage that all mechanical creatures have unlike sensitive human beings.

"Sam, you can't frighten me!" Zenna shouted suddenly flaring up. "Is that a threat you just made, you'll kill me? You better watch that. There's a law against a person who intimidates another".

Sam shook his head disapprovingly and stalked out of the room Zenna's heart skipped a beat, her happiness was seized by agony. I can't believe Sam's now noxious, violence, she thought. What happened to my joy? It has dispersed into smog. Zenna's eyelashes trembled, and the wild throbbing of her heart nearly choked her.

18

CHAPTER EIGHTEEN

Suddenly, Zenna felt a diabolic dislike for Sam, something she'd never had before. The atmosphere was stagnant. Zenna was humiliated and she seemed squashed like a mouse under the foot of a giant. Zenna, alone her head bowed, her shoulders drooping in despair, finally plucked up enough courage to walk out of the kitchen. Like a dying wind, anxiety and fear saturated her. She was in a stupor, dizzy. She tidied up the store, served some early customers and when she was alone, made an effort to read *An American Tragedy* by Theodore Dreiser; but the lines on the page passed under her eyes in vain. Zenna read without understanding a word of it. She finally discarded the book and started knitting on a sweater. All of Zenna's flowers had been torn-up, crushed in the sand, scattered and trampled on. Lately, Zenna was alone she often addressed herself aloud and she expostulated "No one step on my vision."

The neighbors knew about Sam and Beatrice and the brutal treatment that Sam had visited upon his wife lately. They were cold towards Sam and many refused to enter the store when he was at home. Sam's Masonic brother decided to confront Sam about the gossip that were floating the neighborhood.

"How is the business, Brother Sam?" His Masonic brother asked as he softly watched the expression on Sam's face.

"Not too bad." Sam replied with a wiry smile. Sam betrayed nervousness by constantly adjusting the button on his shirt. Masonic brother could see that Sam was nervous and decided to make his move.

"People are talking about you and that young girl." Masonic brother glanced at Sam impassively, and waited for him to answer. Sam gave Masonic brother the tobacco, and wrote the purchase down in the ledger, alongside the numbers he had put in. Sam didn't answer brother.

"People are saying that you're treating your wife mighty bad". The Masonic brother continued. "Everyone around here is crazy about your wife and you know that. Your wife is a good woman, a sweet person. No reflection on you, Brother Sam."

Sam made a rather pitiful attempt to sound debonair. "I don't give a damn about what people say". Sam's voice rose to a crescendo of cruelty. "I'm a man! I never think of what common folks say. Those people don't dictate to me. Poor people are capricious. It is a law of nature. I was once one of them, but I'm different now. I call the shots and that's that". Sam expressed as he closed a button on his shirt, exposing his hairy chest.

"Oh, I'm so sorry, Brother Sam". The Masonic brother apologized. "I didn't know that it had gotten that far. I mean no harm, now. You're still my brother and friend. I just thought that I could help; no hard feelings now. Brother Sam, we're having a meeting tomorrow night. I expect you to be there". The Masonic

brother voiced and hurriedly walked out of the store.

Zenna had been the liaison between the customers who

shopped at their store. Sam kept many neighbors bolita numbers

in by the week. Some evaded payment and Sam had to lean

heavily on the unpunctual patrons.

A jungle atmosphere pervaded the room. Sam marched

into the kitchen after sleeping out all night. Like a bold barbarian

creature, starved for raw meat. Sam ferociously explored.

"Zenna! Let me go!" Zenna's eyes closed slightly, when some-

thing was said and she was sure of its meaning. Zenna made

believe that she didn't hear at all. Sam stared down on Zenna

and suddenly an uncontrollable urge of hatred for her came over

him. Some demon was whispering into Sam's ears, and seeing

Zenna suddenly smiling lips, caused a mad passion to stir within

him. Sam loathed Zenna sitting at the kitchen table eating her

breakfast. How could she eat at a time like this? Zenna's eyes

mocked Sam and at that moment he despised Zenna, more than

anything in the whole world. Sam shook his head and gazed about like an eagle. He knew, that he had to get rid of Zenna, but he didn't know exactly how.

Sam strode over to Zenna, his face contorted and gloomy. He whipped out his pistol from his pocket; he always carried one. Sam raised his arm and pointed the gun at Zenna's head. "Let me go Zenna!" The unblinking gazes of his black eyes were harsh and fixed. "If you don't let me go Zenna, I'll blow your head off, right now." Zenna was like a earthworm impaled with a farmer's rake. Zenna opted to avoid the labyrinth. She jumped up from the table like a scalded cat practically overturning it.

Zenna's eyes were dilated and she was choking for breath. "Don't do it Sam! Sam, you'll be sorry. I'm your wife. A husband shouldn't hurt his wife." Zenna made a dash for the door. Sam gave chase, saliva dripping from his mouth. His light brown, holly ball hair seemed to have waxed together tighter. Sam's long fingers extended like tigers claws in battle. Little tongues were talking in Sam's fragmented veins and his mind and gun emptied.

Two bullets tore into Zenna's back as she tried to escape with her life. She fell to the ground, at the front gate. She turned half-circle and she spat out a massive amount of blood. A weak cry came from Zenna's mouth. She turned on her side and her dainty hands shoot out convulsively, as she clawed the ground.

There was a stifled groan. Zenna's eyes were the bosom of all of her family. Zenna's once distinctive, striking features, her round head with it mass of jet-black hair framing her moon face, surmounted on a small, slender body. Like a drowsy chicken, Zenna cuddled her head and then the life which had sustained her more than forty years ebbed out.

Sam's eyes incoherently rolling wildly, his arms fell to his side paralyzed with terror. For a moment, Sam didn't know what to do, he pocketed the gun, strode down the steps, stepped over his wife's body, clad in a plaid dress with a Bertha collar. Zenna's dress had blow-up to the middle of her thighs.

Sam reached out and opened the gate. When he had reached his car, he took a final look back. He then slouched under the wheel of his Caddie and drove away.

Some of the neighbors heard the report from Sam's gun; the air was charged with electricity. People gathered, convinced at last, that what they heard was factual and they scurried about like rodents in a burning silo.

19

CHAPTER NINTEEN

A boy was dispatched to Aunt Julia's house. He ran hurriedly with bated breath, "Sam just shot Zenna!" He explained excitedly as he dashed back to the crowd. Aunt Julia was gathering flowers for a bouquet, for the house and Uncle Oscar were watering the lawn.

"Oh, my God!" Aunt Julia and Uncle Oscar said in unison. Flowers plummeted to the ground. Uncle Oscar dropped the hose and stumbled over it almost falling to the ground. They went in little sprints, alarm written largely on their faces. They wanted to run, but due to the many summers and their arthritic legs, their strength failed and they went slow passed as though struggling against a gale.

"Oh Lordy!" Aunt Julia clasped her hands beseechingly, as she eyed the catastrophe. Aunt Julia, hysterically fell to the ground and enveloped Zenna's head into her arms, as she rocked back and forth. "Why? Why did you do it Sam?" Someone said. "No Julia, don't touch the body. Wait until the police come". Aunt Julia didn't hear any of that. "Sam, if you didn't want her anymore, you could've brought her back home. We love her Sam, We love her." Aunt Julia moaned pathetically, squeezing the deceased Zenna tighter in her arms, until an officer arrived and untangled Aunt Julia form the body and helped the bloody, sobbing Aunt Julia to her feet.

Uncle Oscar almost choked with anxiety and asthma. You could hear his breathing and wheezing. Uncle Oscar faulted as he reached for the phone, trying to call Rufus in New York. Due to his nervous state, his asthma fit opened up. Uncle Oscar has a history of chronic asthma disorder. As he grew older, disturbance of any triggered the illness and caused prolonged coughing. Thick saliva oozed from Uncle Oscar's mouth and nose. When Uncle Oscar's asthma was really profound, his farts sent out a roar the sounded like firecrackers on the Forth of July. Those attacks left Uncle Oscar weak and with blood shot eyes.

Uncle Oscar was trying to call New York. Operator! Cough - -erru erruyng! New Y- -sneeze, ppppp-fff-tt-tttttt! Krrumff! Whom, New York cough- New York sneeze, ppppp-fff-fart-boom-phtphhhttttt-cough - -whooopppp- - -hummmmmmmmmmmm, sneeze, phtphhhttttttt- -cough- - -whooooooom- - - -cough- - uuuuuuuuuuuuuummmmmm! Uncle Oscar tried to reach Rufus in New York. The operator was con-tinually asking, "Your number please." Finally, Uncle Oscar gave up in disgust. He discovered that the small bottle of medi-cation he carried wasn't on him. He looked in the pantry for whiskey, but Sam has already cleaned out all the drinks. Uncle Oscar amble to the door and beckoned to a teenage boy; he pro-duced a soiled, closely folded piece of paper from is pocket.

"Call this number!" Uncle Oscar requested, as the coughing and farting was now pronounced, "Tell Rufus Zenna is dead! Come at once. She met with an accident." The young boy called and gave the message, then hung up, not allowing Rufus to respond.

Uncle Oscar gave the boy another number to call, Uncle Albert in Savannah, Georgia. Uncle Albert was given the same message and the boy hung up.

Rufus tried to get Sam's number, but the line was busy; the phone was off the hook. Rufus tried Uncle Oscar number, the there was no answer. He tried Uncle Albert's number, the line was busy. Rufus phone Sam's sister, no answer. After a terrifying and distressful moment, Rufus phone Lulu and told her everything.

"It must be a prank," Lulu stated. "I talked to Zenna two day ago and things were fine."

"No, I don't think so." Rufus spoke, a neighbor's boy made the call. I could hear Uncle Oscar coughing in the background. He had an asthma attack and couldn't talk. I'm calling

Uncle Albert again, and if he got the message, then you know that something is wrong. The boy hung up before I could ask him what kind of an accident that Zenna was in. I'm leaving as soon as I can make reservations."

After Lulu tired all the family numbers that she had and didn't get any response, she called Rufus. In the meantime, Rufus had called Uncle Albert and they had gotten the same message. They were leaving by bus, immediately. "What are you going to do?" Rufus inquired, "Shall I make reservations for two?"

"What about Rena Mae?" Lulu asked, "She is our sister too."

"I know that." Rufus spoke harshly, wishing that it were all a bad dream. "I don't know where she lives, do you?"

"No, I called Rena Mae yesterday; her landlady said that she had moved. I also called Kay and she didn't know where she was either."

"Well, there you are." Rufus said. "As soon as I can get a flight out, I'm leaving."

"Very well." Lulu cried softly. "Make it for two.' Rufus and Lulu flew to Jacksonville, Florida, that same day.

A long line had formed. Numerous feet shuffled about. There was new light in the people's eyes, making the wrinkled faces of old, growing with rage and young faces bent on violence. All showing the white of their eyes and forming their heavy lips into circles shouted, "Get that damn running nigger!" Late comers saw the door closed and they were under the impression that Sam was still inside the house. People yelled epithets and insults at the house. There was the continuous roar of catcalls, pierced by screams. "Come out you murderer! You racketeering gangster! Bolita dog! Lynch the bastard." The screams were follows by a sudden move forward. Where the police line was weak, a surge would pop open. As soon as one part was strengthened, the bulge would pop somewhere else. The neighborhood was aghast, nothing like that had ever happened in their section before. People turned out in great numbers, weeping and mumbling.

One man who had at one time owed Sam three-dollars for his weekly number bill, broke through the barrier. "let me get my hands on the greedy son-of-a-bitch!" He shouted as he was restrained at the doorsteps. He had carried a smelting resentment for Sam, since Sam forced him to fork over the money he had hidden away to buy his wife a surprise Mother's Day gift.

Uncle Oscar was extremely irritated to the last degree. Dismal frowns furred his brow. His lips puckered and he rolled his eyes viciously. He shook his fist on the air disapprovingly. Then another glob of spittle flowed over his chin and he wiped it away. "I'd like to twist your tail myself!" Uncle Oscar's repertoire several words was finally strung together. Then, another fit of coughing, as he stood by the ambulance.

"Go home, now!" The sheriff drawled in a loud voice. "You see that he isn't in the house. Now get. You can't take the law into your hands. Get! Get!" The sheriff waved his hand at the gathered crowd as though he was shooing away chickens from a peach tree loaded with ripened peaches. The Jacksonville's Police Department didn't hold good blood for Sam Dorkins anyway. Due to Sam's big number bosses, they couldn't touch him, but now, they knew that justice would triumph.

Sam flew the streets as though he as attacking an enemy, as he stomped the brakes in front of his sister, Daphne's house. He entered Daphne's home with an attaché's case full with money that he had drawn from the bank the day before; without Zenna's knowledge. Sam left only a few hundred dollars and he cleaned the safe that they had secretly installed in the house. When she entered his sister's house, he had a strange look on his face; his eyes bulged, his face was drenched with perspiration and his hands were trembling lightly.

Daphne had just walked in from doing her shopping and she was storing her wares. She turned when she heard the key on the door. "Sam! What's wrong? Are you sick?" Sam didn't answer her; he approached the table and said quietly, watching the effects of each word upon his sister's face. "Keep this sis." Sam

drummed his fingers in the table. "I just killed Zenna, I'll need a

lawyer. Do you have anything in this house to drink? I feel like a

shot." Sam fingered his hard-ball curly hair. He then turned

sideways from the table and crossed his long legs. Same looked

up at his sister. Daphne was still standing there like a stone. "Do

you have anything in this house to drink?" An unmistakable look

of uneasiness and vexation flitted across Daphne's physiog-

nomy. Obviously, her tongue swollen in her mouth spoke for the

first time.

"Sam! Don't you realize what you've done?" Daphne

stared at Sam curiously. "You've murdered your wife, Sam. You

should be on your knees to God. And you sit there asking for a

drink and a lawyer?" Damn that shit you're talking about>" a

strong baritone voice issued from Sam's mouth. Sam's eyes

were convincing, rock like marble in a brass cup. Sam screwed

up one eyes as though taking aim at something at a shooting gal-

lery. "Give me a drink! After I get my drink, I'll turn myself in".

Sam lit a cigarette and narrowed his eyes. "You have the money. Get me out. I'm rich. I won't be held in jail for long!" Daphne swept from the kitchen to the bedroom and retrieve a bottle of liquor from the commode. She returned with the bottle and planked it down on the table with a thump. Sam crouched over the drink and gave Daphne a snake like gaze. "Get me out jail. I'm rich."

"I'll do my best." Daphne answered with a heavy tongue and heart and weeping eyes. "I know you will." Sam swallowed the drink. The whiskey burned the gumball in his mouth. A frown curved over Sam's lips and he looked at his sister, half closing his eyes as he always did when he was tipsy. "Don't fret sis, everything's going to be all right." Sam assured Daphne as she fussed with the dishes in the sink. "Get me out! I was right! Zenna wouldn't let me go." Sam wiped his mouth with the back of his hand. "Zenna, threatened to tie up everything. IMAGINE THAT! Zenna, wanted me to be poor again. I won't stand for that. Zenna wanted to destroy me. All that I've worked so hard for." Sam demanded as he strode out of the house and swooshed away in his Cadillac.

"Sam! Sam!" Daphne called with out –stretched hands, unable to connect her thoughts. Sam paid her no attention to her. He was gone. "Lordy! My brother is crazy." Daphne's eyes closed slightly and her mind finally came to her. It's my fault, she thought. Daphne and her husband raised Sam since he was eight years old, after their mother died. They brought him up with their son, Joel and they thought they had done what was right by Sam. Joel had never done the things that Sam had done. Sam always believed in quick bucks. There was something wrong and evil about Sam and the fast dollar. Sam was adventurous and crafty. He would come up with an answer to a situation when the rest of the family couldn't. Sam was a happy child, but a restless person, Daphne reminisced.

Daphne reached for the phone to call her son Joel, but the line was busy. Sam was always willing to help and he certainly had done more than his share of chores around the house, she recalled. We had lots of fun and pleasure brining up Sam, but it's all gone now. What a mess. Daphne began to cry. My son Joel is different. When he's home, he is jolly and happy and his wife and children are glad to see him. They adore each other. I believe Sam would've been different if he had children. Sam never liked hard work and wouldn't do it; not for long. Sam's personality loved women. When they broke up and the women left town, something seemed to have died inside of Sam. But Sam wasn't really happy until he met and married Zenna. Daphne recalled.

Daphne tried to call Joel a second time,. It was still busy. Daphne was glade Sam had found true love at last. Sam and Zenna had grown together and they attended church together. They had improved so much on the property and they were very happy and prosperous. Until that brazen hussy, Beatrice, put some hoodoo spell on my brother, she thought.

Why did that gal mess up my brother? Beatrice's mother is rich. She is the best designer in this part of town. She sews for the rich white people. She's doing big business. Her mother

don't sew for us poor niggers, we can't pay the price. The prices

she charges to sew for one dress, a person could buy ten dresses

at a bargain store. Beatrice's mother is kept by a rich white man,

a buyer. He built her a ten-room house. These black bitches want

all the money, Daphne thought.

Daphne opened the briefcase; her hands flew up into the

air. "Oh my God!" Daphne exclaimed. "Where did Sam get all

this money? He must've robbed a bank. Joel must come at once!

Daphne spoke as she reached for the phone. Joel's wife an-

swered the phone, but Joel wasn't there. Daphne explained to

Joel's wife what had happened and she must get in touch with

Joel at once. They must come as soon as possible, because Sam

is in big trouble and he needs his family.

20

CHAPTER TWENTY

Sam felt as if a load had been lifted from him. A smile of joy flittered across his face and lingered for a moment. Sam parked his car in a parking lot and quietly strolled up the jail's steps. Sam's memory locked behind him and his madness seemed to have crept like a horrible disease over his whole being. His eyes were cunning, his lips dropped, and his nostrils were fluted. Sam's massive fuzzy hair stood at attention. His long fingers extending and he had all the symptoms of a mad man.

"I'm Sam Dorkins! I came to give myself up." Sam spoke to the desk clerk. "I've just killed my wife. We had a fight

and the gun accidentally went off. I have a permit for the gun."
Sam produced the pistol and the permit.

The clerk glanced through the pile of warrants that was
before him. "Sam Dorkins!" The clerk read the name twice and
smiled faintly. "Oh yes. Yes, but your wife was shot in the back,
at the gate. Seems to me, she was running for her life. Is that
right?"

"Like I said, we had a fight." Sam repeated. "The re-
volver went off accidentally." Sam adjusted his collar, stroked
his chin, and raised his eyes. "Like I said, it was an accident."
Sam showed no remorse at all about what he had done.

"We're looking for you." The clerk continued. "We have
a warrant for your arrest. You were wise to come in." The officer
beckoned to a policeman who was busy at the far side of the
room. "This man is Sam Dorkins, book him for murder." A faint
sense of having taken part in some strange tragedy came over
Sam. There was the reality of a nightmare about the whole thing.
Sam cocked his head to one side and answered the imaginary

voice. "You're not my wife Zenna. I've just divorced you."
Thinking about Zenna stung Sam to the bones and he groaned as
he was in agony in his jail cell. Sam got up and pace the cell,
scowling darkly. His heart throbbing wildly and he couldn't
keep his mind fixed on any one thing. Sam's illusions had raised
a terrible, fearful conscience. In his mind, there were visible
phantoms before him, at all times.

Shadows of his crime peered at him from silent corners.
Mocked him from secret places, whispering, nonessentials into
his ears. Wherever Sam was, frigid fingers prodded him. "Oh my
God! I believe I'm going crazy." Sam thought. Sam heard small
voices. "You're crazy Sam." Zenna voice said. "Oh my, I've
murdered my wife." Sam shrieked, "I begged you for months to
leave me Zenna. But you wouldn't. No one will stand in my way
Zenna. It was an accident. I'm rich. I'm justified in what I've
done. I'm justified! I love Beatrice so much. She is so young and
beautiful. Where is that God Damn lawyer?"

"Pipe down in there." The clerk called out. Sam gave no heed or was too far gone to hear the clerk.

"I must get out of here!" Sam yelled loudly. "Beatrice! Where are you? I'm coming Beatrice! Beatrice! Beatrice! My sweet, Beatrice. I'll get out and marry you." Like a clock's pendulum, Sam's mind swung back and forth. "Zenna, I'll kill you if you stand in my way,' Sam expostulated, pacing the floor. "I'm going to marry you Beatrice."

An illusion, answered Sam. "No you won't Sam. I'm your wife Zenna, remember? You're my husband and don't forget it."

"No! No! You're not my wife. I've divorced you, Zenna. When we first met you were young, sweet, and pretty. I loved you then, but now that's past and I don't want to think about it anymore."

There was silence, the two clerks looked at each other and smiled. "Go see if he's asleep or dead from a heart attack.' As soon as the junior clerk started to move, "Bang! Bang!' Sam shouted as he ran about firing a mythical gun at the echoes. "Zenna, you're not my wife. I just divorced you!" Thousands of voices were babbling at Sam and he couldn't understand why they wouldn't stop. The chatter was maddening to the other inmates. The desk clerk, guard, and the doctor entered Sam's cell; after a struggle, an injection was administered.

The murder of Zenna had simply been a deranged mind of the moment. After Sam awoke, few random thoughts filtered through his mind. Certainly, he wouldn't be sentenced for an accident. Didn't he have a permit to carry a gun? He is rich! He had done the right thing when he took most of the money out of the bank, Sam thought. Daphne would make sure that he wouldn't be out of circulation, long. Beatrice would wait for him; she had too. Where would she find another rich man? No, he didn't have anything to worry about, Sam thought.

The night was clear and tranquil. There was a half moon that floated in the dim light and the gray clouds scurried hastily by. Heavy dew had fallen during the night and the cool breeze was blowing in and the flicker of purpose stirred in Sam. Sam got up and took his coat and walked to the pigeon-hole window. He felt a draft. He went to the bed and took a soiled army blanket with a hole in the middle. Sam draped it around his stately shoulders and began to pace his cell. "I was justified in what I've done." Sam bellowed, his mind fluctuating. "Let me go Zenna or I'll kill you." Sam pointed the imaginary gun and started firing. "Daphne! Where are you? Get me out of here! Get me out!" "Pipe down in there!" the guard ordered the second time, as he passed Sam's cell. He saw Sam garbed in the blanket.

Buddhist Monk, the keeper visualized. Sam gazed into the guard's eyes. The gaze of his own closet evil little eyes were sad. A nasty smile stole into Sam's features, and he began breathing fast and hard. Muffled voices kept sneaking up on Sam, but he smiled contemptuously, rocking, on his heels. Sam wrinkled his old furrowed brow and picked his nose. "Let me go Zenna or I'll kill you." Sam became verbal again, tormenting Zenna.

During the evening, Daphne, Sam's lawyer, and the family were at Sam's cell, but he was sedated. Later that evening, when they returned to Sam's cell, one look at Sam and the family knew that his mental faculty was out of control.

He began to rage and he didn't recognize his family. It was decided that Sam would be transferred to Jacksonville's City Mental Ward. Sam was still ranting continuously until he was restrained. The Ward's psychology, theory, was to let the patient express themselves vocally. Sam was like an electric doll, wound up. He not only expressed himself vocally, but he began to bang on the door and wall. Sam was like a giant fish just taken out of the water. He struck out in all directions, kicking wildly, like a wrestler. He eluded his captors for a while, but finally he was backed into a corner and a heavy white cloth was thrust over his shoulders. But they still had to deal with his legs. When they at last put Sam into a tub-like receptacle, epithets flew from Sam's mouth in volumes. One attendant reached into his pocket for wadding for Sam's mouth. Sam seemed to perceive the intention like a Cobra, a slight turn of the head and Sam's teeth caught the side of the attendant's hand. He drew his hand back and glanced down at the blood gushing out like oil from a well. "The son-of-a-bitch bit me!" The attendant spoke, still watching the flow of blood.

"Well, what're you waiting for?" One keeper exclaimed. "You better go to the doctor. That wretch may have rabies." They chuckled, as one aide strode to the door to let the wounded one out.

"We need to put this swab on a long stick for that fuck-er." One helper voiced. "Stick my ass, we need a ten-foot pole", the other aide said. "Do you know who he is?" One asked. "No, but I know that he is a crazy son-of-a-bitch."

One aide spoke. "That's the big wheel, Sam Dorkins. And to think, when I was a boy I wanted to he like this prick. Just about every poor boy that knew him, wanted to be like him. His fine clothes, shiny new Caddie, pocket full of money, and pussies fighting over him and chasing his ass all over town."

"With all the money and pull," exclaimed another aide. "What he want to go crazy for. Man, I would stay around and use that money." It's pussy man, pussy." Another expresses. "To much of that stuff will run any man crazy. Pussy had has a way of getting a man mixed up. Especially, if he thinks someone is getting some of it. I say to hell with the cunt. A little, but, not too much."

After Sam was restrained they stood for a while and watched him squirm like a snake impaled under a car's wheel. About this time news was circulating all over town. Beatrice's mother frightened about the whole episode packed Beatrice off to relatives in Key West, Florida.

It was night when the plane taxied-down in Jacksonville. The wide expansion of the bright sky lit up the town. A Silver Star moon shone out from behind the clouds. The stars started lighting up one after the other, so that they seemed to close in on you. There were so many of them that it was impossible to see anything else. The air was thick with sweet, fresh cut grass. Then the realization of the time dawned on Rufus and Lulu.

They took a cab to Aunt Julia's house. They heavily plodded up the stairs and rang the bell. While they were waiting, Rufus glanced through the window. The dogs were gleaming with almost human curiosity. The ceiling chandelier shed a bright light throughout the room. After a sad greeting, they sat. They were choked with emotions as they realized the truth, which was divesting indeed. "Where is Rena Mae?" Aunt Julia inquired.

"We couldn't find her." Rufus answered. "Rena Mae moves about so frequently. Aunt Julia, what happened?" Rufus spoke sadly.

"Oh Rufus, I don't know where to begin." Aunt Julia said. "Sam shot Zenna in the back. She was running for her life. It's a long story, Rufus. Sam had been seeing a young girl, I was told."

"That's the God's truth, Rufus." Uncle Oscar spoke softly, being mindful of his asthma attack; and any excitement would trigger a blast.

"The girl was just seventeen years old." Aunt Julia stated. "And the gal turned Sam's head completely around. I questioned Zenna about what I heard, but she said that it was all gossip. Zenna said that they were getting alone just fine. So I couldn't press the issue further."

"Why did Zenna want to hide the matter?" Uncle Albert asked. "I don't know," Aunt Julia stated.

"Maybe Zenna didn't want to worry her family." Aunt Callie spoke hurriedly. "Zenna had a bad experience with her first husband. She probably thought that she wasn't going to bring her family into the situation."

"That's very well could be." Aunt Julia said. "The body can be viewed at six o'clock tomorrow evening. Sam is just about mad, Daphne said. Sam gave himself up. He is in the city's mental ward. You can see him tonight, but I don't think he'll recognize you. Daphne said that Sam don't know her."

Rufus put his face into his hands and cried. Rufus thought about the first marriage and how it ended. "How is it possible that a person as good as Zenna had bad husbands?" He questioned. "I'll visit Sam in the hospital. I just want to ask him one question; why did you shoot my sister in the back?"

"I'm not going to the hospital." Lulu flared up. "I don't want to see the mad dog!" Lulu fell into Aunt Julia's arms and they wept grievously. Uncle Albert and Aunt Callie said that they weren't going to the hospital either.

Rufus took a cab to the hospital, alone. After he explained to the personnel that Sam was his brother-in-law, he was allowed to see Sam.

Sam had stopped talking and he wasn't sedated. Sam seemed to be in space. His eyes were set and his mouth agape. When Rufus reached Aunt Julia's house, he explained Sam's condition to the family. Rufus has spoken to the doctor and he said that Sam probably would last through the night; and every-one seemed pleased about that.

Aunt Julia had called Daphne and her family. She told them that Rufus, Lulu, Uncle Albert, and Aunt Callie had arrived. Daphne and her family went over to Aunt Julia's house. They talked and cried until late in to the night. Daphne was brokenhearted about it all. Sam had really been happy with Zenna and settled down, until he met that brazen Beatrice, she thought.

Around four o'clock that morning, Aunt Julia's telephone rang; it was Daphne. Sam had died from a cerebrum blockage. Now, it would be two funerals. Sam and Zenna were buried side by side, one headstone for both. The family decided that was the proper way. Daphne gave Sam and Zenna a very expensive burial. At the church, Rufus glanced resolutely, like a cow on a rope dragged himself toward the bier. The church was packed and some of the people mourned in the churchyard. The crowd hung in cluster over Zenna and Sam's bier, leaning on one another with inquisitive eyes.

CHAPTER TWENTY

Rufus stood by Zenna's coffin, a shudder ran across his quivering lips, his head twitched slowly as he stared in frantic perplexity at Zenna.

After the burial, the family assembled at Sam's and Zenna's house. Daphne had told them about the money that Sam took from the bank and deposited it with her. Daphne paid the lawyer, hospital, and burial cost. Sam and Zenna made no will, but they found a deposit book with Kay Hannibal's name on it. Zenna had established the funds shortly after she was married to Sam. The family decided that the house, store, and the Cadillac were to be sold and the money divided among the family.

The family also resolved that they could choose whatever they wanted from Sam's and Zenna's personal items. Rufus took the sterling silver place setting for twelve. He also brought his wife Zenna's wrist watch. Rufus packed all Zenna's poems and took them to New York. He collected some sweaters that Zenna had made, wool and was crocheted by hand. Lulu took Zenna's typewriter for her daughter Mitzy. She also chose the crystal, set of twelve, and a cashmere black coat with Sable collar.

Sam's cuff links set, tie pin, watches, Zenna's hat, dresses, scarves, gloves, and shoes was distributed among the rest of the family.

21

CHAPTER TWENTY ONE

Rena Mea had found a new love interest and the two were locked away in Rena's Mae room for two weeks. When the love vacation was over, he went back to work. That same day, Rena Mae decided she would take a stroll on 125th Street. Rena Mae met on of her down home friends. "You didn't go to your sister's funeral?" The friend asked. "What sister's funeral?" Rena Mae exclaimed. "Didn't you know? Sam shot Zenna in the back. Zenna is dead. Rufus and Lulu went down a week ago. My sister wrote and told me about it."

Rena Mae didn't want to hear anymore or thank the good woman. She ran wildly through the streets screaming. Then realized she was attracting attention. Rena Mae stopped promptly. "I must leave at once for Jacksonville." She spoke aloud. Suddenly, like an explosion of gun powder, the idea of money flashed through her head. "Oh, my God! I don't have enough money for the trip." She said. With ill concealed desperation, Rena Mae dashed into a bar, and headed to the bathroom to count her money. Rena Mae counted eight dollars total. "This isn't enough," she spoke aloud. A woman waiting to get to her bathroom asked, "What did you say?" Rena Mae paid no heed to her. "My relief check won't come until next month." Rena Mae was still talking to herself, aloud. What am I going to do? What can I pawn? My watch and television are in the repair shop, she thought. Finally, a tearful Rena Mae came out of the bathroom and into the streets. She kept turning over in her mind how she could obtain the money for the trip. My daughter Kay just had a baby a month ago, they don't have any money.

When Rena Mae had lathered the street with her tears, it-dawned on her that maybe, just maybe, Lulu left her fare at the beauty shop. As she approached the parlor, she saw a sign in the window. "Zenna is dead. We could not find you." Like a well-trained mastiff, Rena Mae entered the shop. Maggie met Rena Mae; they embraced, "I'm sorry Rena Mae." Maggie consoled. "But where were you all this time?"

"I just moved to a new address." Rena Mae stated, teary-eyed. "My boyfriend was on vacation and we stayed in. Now, he has gone back to work. Did Lulu leave my fare?" "No, she did not." Maggie said. "Maggie, do you have any money that I may borrow?" Rena Mae pleaded. "You know that I will pay you back."

"No, I do not," Maggie stated, looking into her purse. "I have less that ten dollars." "Does my sister have any money in the shop?" Rena Mae asked pathetically. "I must leave for Jacksonville today." "Yes, Lulu have some money here." Maggie explained. "But, if I give you that money, I must have an 'I owe you", because I must replace this money."

"Alright, I will give you an 'I owe you'." Rena Mae said anxiously. "I must get to Jacksonville today."

When Rena Mae arrived in Jacksonville, Zenna and Sam were already buried and Rufus and Lulu had left for New York.

"Rena Mae, what made you so late?" Aunt Julia asked. "I was away with a friend and I did not get the message until I got back" Rena Mae explained.

"Sam and Zenna are buried together." Aunt Julia stated. "Sam is dead too?' Rena Mae asked. "Yes, Sam had a cerebrum blockage." Uncle Oscar answered. "The blood wasn't getting to his brain properly and this is why he turned from Zenna to that young girl. Sam's brain wasn't getting the right amount of blood.."

"I am glad that Sam is dead too." Rena Mae spoke harshly. "Sam killed my good sister. Zenna has never done any-thing to harm anyone. After I rest and change my clothes, I want to go to my sister's grave." I will take you." Aunt Julia said. "Zenna and Sam are buried side by side. Oh, Rena Mae, it was a sad affair. The church could not hold the people. Just as many people on the outside of the church as it was inside.

Rena Mae was saddened and began to cry. She was very hurt because she didn't get to see her sister before she was buried. But she settled for photos of Zenna and Sam in their biers at the church. Rena Mae placed a wreath on her sister's grave and also sent up a prayer for her. Rena Mae wept and begged Zenna to forgive her for not being there before she was buried. Rena Mae was glad that she was not there, because she did not want to see that bastard Sam. I am glad that he is dead, she thought again.

After Rena Mea and Aunt Julia had visited the grave, they stopped by Daphne's house. Then they went to Sam's and Zenna's house. Rena Mae was told that Rufus, Lulu, and the rest of the family had taken all the best articles. Rufus took the silver set and other items, and Lulu carried the typewriter, cashmere coat, and some other pieces.

"Rufus and Lulu said that they could not find you." Aunt Julia explained. "They could have found me if they wanted too." Rena Mae spoke angrily. Rena Mae rummaged through the house, but she didn't find much. Some old faded dresses of Zenna's, worn towels and sheets. "Rufus and Lulu, the dirty bastards; they wanted all my sister's thing for themselves>"

"Rena Mae I do not think so." Aunt Julia corrected. "We got what we wanted. No one was fighting over anything."

"Well, what is Mitzy going to do with a typewriter?" Rena Mae expressed. "She can't type. My daughter Kay can type. Kay had academic training. She types up her reports on her job."

Rena Mae was left out of everything. She blamed Rufus and Lulu for it all. She was fuming, but the anger didn't last long. She had to humble herself and call Rufus to wire her fare for the Greyhound Bus.

Although Rena Mae knew that Aunt Julia and Uncle Albert would loan her the money, she didn't want them to know she was broke. Rena Mae sat in Aunt Julia's house, reminiscing. Her life was much the same as it was when she lived on Zubly Street in Yamacraw. Rena Mae still depended on her family for help when an emergency arrived.

As Rena Mae sat, memories of the old homestead in Savannah, Georgia had been erased. The house where Rufus and the three sisters were brought up in was no more. The whole district in Yamacraw gave way to an expressway. Margie had moved to the Savannah Sugar Refinery area. Margie and her husband bought a house, a four-bedroom house. Margie wasn't juggling bottles anymore. She devoted her time to her family, home, gardening, church, and community service. Her father had died and her mother, now, lived with her.

Zulby Street and that area was now enlarged to become a part of the railroad station; as well as Maryland's Fried Chicken, Fish, and Shrimp, Burger King, Standard Chevron, some housing projects, and some churches. All that were left in the immediate area was the Star Theater. The movie house was a

325

little cleaner than during The Depression days, but still, was not

up to the health code.

22

CHAPTER TWENTY TWO

When Rufus and Lulu taxied down to J.F.K., they took a cab. Lulu was dropped off and Rufus continued to his home. Rufus alighted from the cab and you could hear his footsteps sounding on the pavement. Junior opened the door and grabbed his dad around the neck, almost knocking him over. After their greeting, Rufus sat down; he felt exhausted, body and soul.

"You must be tried, dear." Dorothy spoke. "I'll fix you a drink."

"Thank you darling. Yes, I'm spent." Rufus stated. Junior began bombarding his father with questions.

"Give your father time to get settled." His mother pleaded. "Your father is weary." After a drink, Rufus had loosened up, and then began to explain the disaster.

When the suitcase was opened, Rufus gave Junior a new whipcord sweater that Zenna had made for Sam and he never wore it. Rufus presented Dorothy with a sterling silver set and the wrist watch. "Junior, some day this silver will be yours," Rufus spoke up, "when we are dead, of course." Junior, trying on his sweater, turned around and gazed blankly at his father as though he was joking.

"You and Mom will never die." Junior said smiling and still unpacking. "Sam went crazy, stone crazy. Mad! Mad! Uncle Sam went crazy? Junior exclaimed excitedly. "I can't picture Uncle Sam going crazy. He drove that Cadillac with one hand. I believe Uncle Sam could drive that Caddie blind folded."

"Yes, I know". Rufus returned. "Sam was an excellent driver. But the mind is just a thin thread, Junior. And it can snap anytime. Of course, the body plays a big part in the mind staying in place. Unusually, a healthy body produces a fruitful mind. But it hasn't been determined what was wrong with Sam's body."

"Look! Mom, Dad," Junior remarked all fidgety and excited, about things his dad had brought back for himself, "Aunt Rena Mae, got whatever, was left. She did not go down with us." Rufus said. She is gone down there now." Junior spoke, "Mama called the beauty shop and Maggie said that Aunt Rena Mae got there." Junior returned. "Dad, what happened to all Aunt Zenna's and Uncle Sam's other things?" Junior wanted to know. "Well, Sam's people had to share in the property." Rufus assured Junior. "Daphne raise Sam; she and the family had to share in what was there, too." "Well, I certainly could have used that Caddie." Junior stated profoundly. "Dad, why didn't you get the Caddie?" "I got what I wanted." Rufus continued, "I just wanted some mementos of my sister and get the hell out of that place. It was too painful."

The sun rolled quietly through the still blue sky and the clouds swiftly floated under it. They seemed to know where they were going and now Rufus was sure where he was headed. As grieved as Rufus was, he found himself a few thousands dollar richer. Rufus had always kept insurance on all of the family. The surety that Rufus would receive, he would make a down payment on a house. That way, he'd always have a real legacy from his sisters. Ma Sybil said to keep the policy on all the family and especially Rena Mae.

The night, Dorothy asked Craig and his wife over to welcome Rufus back. The salutation was short and infinitely restrained. It was as though, it was a bankrupt protocol, in a sustained note of music. They expressed their condolences.

At first, things were a little strained, but after Dorothy had supplied the guest with strong drinks, tongues became loose. Rufus explained everything about the sorrowful incident. They sat dewy eyed and were saddened about what happened. The guests stayed until midnight.

That night, in bed, Rufus reached over pulling Dorothy into his arms. "I thought, I wouldn't ever feel anything warm again." Rufus said. "You mean you died on me!" Dorothy declared, with humor that was pushing through the crown of their isolation.

"Not anymore, baby." Rufus grabbed Dorothy greedily into his arms. "Baby! Now, I'm alive. Come, come to Papa!" Dorothy flashed back with a broken laugh. Her smile had opened naturally. Then she finished with a subdued yap, like a puppy. "Mama's is so glad to have Papa back." Dorothy said kissing Rufus hungrily.

After breakfast, they sat at the table, talking. "How would you like to have a house in Westchester, New York?" Rufus smiled faintly.

"What; a house in the suburbs?" Junior laughed with enthusiasm, as intriguing as the Asiatic Flute. "I could have a dog and we can get a new care like Uncle Sam's car, huh, huh, huh, Dad?" "A dog, maybe." Rufus spoke, "A car, maybe, but not like Uncle Sam's car. He drove a Cadillac. Sam was a Cadillac hound. He could afford a Cadillac. His kind of work warranted it. Sam's work was light and very lucrative. I have to break my

back for my money. I will be glad to own any car, if it was a

good car. Junior, you must go to college and college costs a lot

of money."

"What do you think about the idea, Dorothy; the house?

You haven't said a word." How can I get a word in?" Dorothy

said smiling broadly. "Junior has the floor."

"Oh, Mom!" Junior expressed piously, deciding to eat

the last doughnut. "I think it's a wonderful idea." Dorothy brigh-

tened. "And I welcome it."

To keep peace in the family, Kay never mentioned that

she was in touch with the Starks, but she told Lulu and Rufus.

Kay's husband was in training to become a motorman for the

Rapid Transit and Kay was training to be a Registered Nurse.

Months after Zenna's death, Kay received a letter informing her

that her Aunt Zenna had left her $10,000. Kay and her husband

were really surprised and excited and were glad that this had

come about. Rufus and Lulu were also glad for Kay, but when

Rena Mae heard about it, she was bitter. "Why didn't Zenna leave $5000 for me and $5000 for Kay?" Rena Mae stated. I don't think any of my family loves me, not even Kay. I have done so much for Kay, too; she thought.

Kay had met her paternal father, Rena Mae saw to that. Kay was not close to her father either. One of her half-brothers had kept in touch with Kay, but they never were devoted to each other.

When the check was deposited to Kay and her husband's account, they knew that they were on their way to Savannah, Georgia as soon as the check cleared. Kay, her husband, and children spent their vacation in Savannah. They didn't tell anyone where they were going. No one knew until they were back. Rufus and Lulu thought Kay was going to visit people who had been so dear to her, was quite admirable.

Dan and Lizzie Starks still lived in the same place where Kay was brought up; the same three-room flat, the swing on the front porch, and a large backyard. When they arrived, Kay dashed from the cab with the baby in her arms and placed the baby into Mama Starks' arms. Lizzie was startled. She was sitting in her porch swing. That was a happy occasion for the whole family. Papa Starks went for their sons, wives, and grandchildren. After the greeting, they talked until late that night. The next day, Kay prepared a big cookout in the back yard. Uncle Albert and Aunt Callie were invited. Kay brought presents for the entire family. When Kay was a child, whenever she met Uncle Albert on the street, he would give her a dollar and she never forgot that. Kay gave Mama and Papa $1000, and she gave her brothers some money also.

When Kay and her family arrived back to New York, she felt exonerated. She called Uncle Rufus and Aunt Lulu and told them about the trip to Savannah. Later that day, Kay called her birth mother. Rena Mae had already heard about the trip, the cousin who Rena Mae had kept in touch with had written her. "I guess you gave your mother half of the money!" Rena Mae stated. "You could have told me that you were going to Savannah. I would have gone with you. I hold no grudge, now."

"No, I didn't give Mama half of the money." Kay answered. "And besides, we wanted to be alone. I bought you a dress in Savannah, a very expensive dress. I do hope you will like it." Rena Mae laughed that tight laugh when something exciting or surprising is happening.

"When do you want me to pick it up?" Rena Mae asked, eager to see what the dress looked like and too hoping that Kay was going to give her some of the money that she received from Zenna's death.

Kay sat on a chair; she was still on the phone and she began reminiscing about circumstances in the past. Did Rena Mae think that she could turn me against Mama; or that I would forget my family? When I was five years old, I had German measles. Mama said that I was unconscious for two days. Papa brought the doctor and he left medicine. The doctor told Mama to keep the room dark and closed. The visit was two dollars.

When everyone had cleaned their pockets, they finally produced two dollars. The doctor was compassionate for the family. On his way out, he left fifty cents on the table. Mama said that when I awoke I looked about. "Mama!" I finally spoke.

"Right here baby!" Mama said. "How do you feel?" I opened my eyes wider, and there Mama was sitting in a chair right by my bed.

"I feel fine." I answered. "I'm hungry!" "Good!" Mama said. "Would you like some hot chicken soup?" "Yes, that will be swell Mama." I replied, trying to get up. "No! No! Don't get up. Mama will bring the soup to you." Mama expressed.

Where was Rena Mae at that time? Maybe someplace, somewhere having a good time with her lovers. I don't condemn Rena Mae for what she did, but how she did it. I can remember one Christmas, Rena Mae sent me a dress and that is all she ever gave me. Mama said that Rena Mae never sent any money or anything. Oh, well! I will buy her a garment or two, once in a

CHAPTER TWENTY TWO

while. I will never give her any of the money that Aunt Zenna

left me; Kay decided.

23

CHAPTER TWENTY THREE

Rufus had escalated himself through his intelligence and assiduous labor, to the level of upper class American. Rufus purchased a house in Westchester, New York. After the movers had deposited the wares, Rufus called Junior V and asked him to bring a broom. Rufus began to sweep away the trash left by the movers. A male bird importantly chasing a female to the telephone wire, took alarm at the shouts that Rufus made. The birds flew away, agitated, protesting indignantly.

As Rufus stood on the front porch with his family, a six month old brown male German Sheppard named True Boy, stood there with them. The sparrows were building their nest in

338

the eves of the house and trees for the right of life, love and fertility. The mounds of green grass grew from the earth, displaying new life, and for a certainty, it was spring.

Rufus went into the bathroom and locked the door. He stood at a large Venetian window and then opened it. He stood there quietly, rubbing his thumb against his fingers as if sampling Japanese silk. Rufus was pondering the circumstances of the past. He smiled and then ambled back to the porch.

"I wish that Aunt Zenna was here." Junior spoke smiling. "She would see our big house, beautiful dog, and lovely surroundings." Junior began to cry. "I loved Aunt Zenna. I'm sorry that she is dead."

"Now son," Rufus consoled, "Now is the time to tell you that every family experience death. My father and mother, Grandpa Phillip, Ma Sybil, and now Zenna are all gone. Only five of the originals are still alive. A person must go on living. Zenna didn't deserve two bad marriages that were worse than Job. Job did live to recover a new family and all the other sub-

stances and was happy from then on. A quote from Maya An-
gelo wrote: 'People at their best are no good.' But there are some
good people. Zenna was one of them, and me, I'm good. I have
never harmed anyone, only when Zenna's first husband
wounded her. I have paid for that and I have learned my lesson.
Only about 20% of the people on the world are really good. The
80% are the troublemakers and wicked. It would take AESOP to
figure that one out.

People are prone to trouble from the day they cry to the
day they die. We must go on. We must try. Trouble should
strengthen us. The grass grows over the grave, time heals the
hurt, the wind blows away the tracks in the sand, and the seasons
take away the pain for he memory of our departed. Life is brief
and no one picks the flowers forever."

"Yes, Dad. I will remember." Junior stated softly. Rufus
walked into the house and stood by the door, looking out. He
broke onto a simple boyish grin that wrinkled the corners of his
eyes. As Rufus stood there, he saw little rosy clouds, as gay as a

maidens smile, and tiny slip of the moon gleamed toward the inaccessible distance.

Rufus walked to the front porch, he felt restless but very secure. He began to think about the family; Uncle Albert and Aunt Callie made it, Uncle Oscar and Aunt Julia made it, Lulu and her husband Harold Jones are making it also. I am still working, so is my wife. And we will make it too. Rena Mae, well, she is receiving her relief check. I guess she will make it also, in her own way. Rufus shook his fist toward the south, in bold opposition.

"Yamacraw! Yamacraw! All you ever gave me was birth." Rufus shouted aloud. "Yamacraw! Yamacraw! Yamacraw! I have beaten you. Look my fabulous house, my family, my dog. It took a long time and lots of hard work; but, I have beaten you Yamacraw! Yamacraw; I have beaten you!"

THE END